SIDEWALK SALE ACROSS AMERICA

A PRESCRIPTION FOR SMALL BUSINESS RE-COVERY FROM COVID, with a Hopeful Ending

Peg Nichols

A story told in participants point of view by chapters

D1710558

We are nature.
We work to improve our lot.
We work to be our best selves, our best nature.
But we are nature.
And nature claims us.
Through time, through hazard, through illness and even
pandemic.
Bless all who have endured Covid.
Pray for those who we've lost and those who've suffered.
They are us.

– your humble scribe,
Spring 2021
Vinland, Kansas

If there is to be a new normal, why not a Better Normal?

SABRINA

Chapter One

I haven't seen Mrs. Reynolds for months, maybe over a year. I wonder if she ever finished the meow-cat sweater she was making for her granddaughter."

With a fork Sabrina Harkins speared a waffle from the waffle iron and slid it onto a large plate. "Do you want a half or a whole?" she asked her husband. What Harold did not want, Nathan or Elsbeth would eat when they finally showed up at the breakfast table.

"Half," without looking up. Harold was studying the tiny lit window of a small radio transceiver, a handi-talky, an HT. He brushed his sandy brown hair away from his forehead. The ham radio network chatter on the transceivers crackled back and forth. Harold was intently following the on-the-air-conversation to see who was up and on-the-air this morning. For the rest of the house it was comforting morning background noise. It beat the cable news in the Harkins' house.

Sabrina added two strips of crisp bacon to a waffle half. Cautiously, she moved two other small transceivers to make room for Harold's breakfast plate. She suspected the transceiver in her husband's hand was a recent purchase Harold had not yet told her about. Money was tight. It might be getting tighter. The

1

Covid-19 Pandemic was a long way from over. It had already infected the world; showing no real promise of letting up.

Harold divided his attention long enough to take a bite of waffle and bacon in front of him on the breakfast table. Harold was obviously proud of his ham radio Technician Class license. This was the first of three license classes – Technician, General, and Extra. He enjoyed the portable connection to the rest of the world. He was a diligent participant in the amateur radio networking and conversations. The technician's exam had been fairly easy to pass; the next test, the general license exam, was going to be a bit more challenging.

". . . come to think of it, I haven't heard from Mrs. Newquist, either," Sabrina continued. She could remember the last time in early spring last year when Elizabeth's Yarn Place had been full of crafters, before the malevolent Covid virus had arrived causing her to wonder if her business was even going to survive . . . financially . . . mentally . . . or even physically. She worried too, of course, about her family, but fought to keep those fears far below the surface; better that neither Harold nor the children catch worry – or Covid – from her. Fear permeated Sabrina's entire atmosphere.

"Or Sally Voyles, she runs a hair salon, and knits red scarves for the hospital cancer program." Chip Q, whose name Sabrina held in secret, came quickly to mind as well. The fascinating young man who pretended it was his wife who did the knitting, he was 'only his wife's non-knitting errand boy'. The list of absent customers – not just customers but knitting friends – was uncomfortably long. And the list seemed to be growing each week.

"What was Mrs. Newquist knitting?" Harold asked absent mindedly. Frowning, Harold turned his attention back to slowly punching frequency numbers into the handi-talky keypad. The ham net had started, so Harold needed to shift frequency in order not to interfere with the net, and to hear the rest of what KØZETA and WA7SCHU were saying about traffic on the west end of town. Hams addressed each other by their call signs instead of their names. Harold was headed west when he left the house.

"Something very unusual. She wouldn't show me. And she wasn't knitting – it was needlepoint." Sabrina wasn't a needle-pointer herself; but she had added needlepoint canvases and threads to her yarn shop inventory because there was no other supply source for a couple of hundred miles. She needed the sales and the happy customers. She saw it as business survival. She had intended, before the Pandemic, to undertake a project for herself, primarily to learn some of the techniques. She knew that if she added needlepoint supplies to her inventory, the "how-do-I?" questions would surely follow. She would need to know and be able to explain the How-To also.

Harold suddenly placed the HT on the table and began to rapidly eat his breakfast. "Who am I taking where this morning?" he asked like someone coming just awake. Simultaneously with the question both Nathan, twelve years old and a seventh-grader, and Elsbeth, five years old and a kindergartner, elbowed each other into the room just squeezing through the kitchen door. If Nathan's light brown hair were much longer, it might match Elsbeth's blond ponytail. Elsbeth was the family's own baby-name. Short for Elizabeth, the given name for Sabrina's own long-past mother. Nathan's hair was looking shaggier than Harold's; maybe she should look for the hair trimmer she had used when he was younger; perhaps Harold would submit to the same treatment. It would save some money.

Hastily, Sabrina poured more batter onto the waffle iron. She cut the half waffle which Harold had not wanted into quarters and put each on a separate plate. Was today the day Nathan went to Overlake Middle School for seventh-grade in-person classes? Or should Harold drop him off at his grandmother's for on-line sessions? Did Elsbeth, a kindergartner at Overlake Elementary, get taken to school? Or would she go with Sabrina to be at the yarn shop at eleven o'clock? It was so hard to keep track of the schedule, even for only two children. How in the world did the family across the street with six children, including twins whom the school district had decided to place in separate classes, keep everything straight?

Harold lifted his coffee mug. "Any refills?" He waited until Sabrina had filled his favorite mug, World's Biggest Ham on one side, World's Greatest Dad on the other, in kid happy colors. "Who is going where today?" He glanced back and forth between Nathan and Elsbeth. "Looks like you kids would help your mother keep track of your schedule." He downed his coffee while he waited for an answer.

"Nathan doesn't like to go to Nana's," Elsbeth piped up.

Nathan looked at his sister with an angry stare. "That's not true," as only an older brother could say to a tattling little sister.

"Yes, you do. You told me. Because she makes you stick to your lessons."

"That's enough of that," Harold said. He unfolded his lanky frame and got up from the table. He put his empty mug in the dishwasher and vanished down the hall and into the part of his and Sabrina's bedroom he called his radio shack. The shack was anywhere a ham radio station was set up. It could be in the basement, separate outdoor shed, or an attic area.

Sabrina turned off the waffle iron. "Finish your breakfast. It is Nathan's day to go to Nana's and your day, Elsbeth, to go to the shop with me." She hoped she had remembered correctly. At any rate, Nathan was always welcome at his grandmother's, strict martinet that she could be, and it would be better than Harold dropping him off at school on a day when he wasn't supposed to be there. "We'll have time," she told Elsbeth, "to go to the grocery store before we need to be at the shop. Here . . ." she handed Elsbeth a notepad . . . "help me make a list."

Harold came back into the kitchen and without breaking stride called to Nathan. "Come on, buddy, the bus is leaving the station." He took his tan jacket with the vending company's logo from the coat rack near the door. He patted the jacket pockets, located his keys and his face mask, and put both in a pocket. Harold would check-in on the net once he was on the way to work.

Nathan gulped down the last of his orange juice. "It's scouts tonight. Are we going to zoom again?"

"We sure are," Harold called from the garage. "Do you think you could learn to be a zoom master? Might even qualify you for another badge." Their voices were lost in the opening of the garage door. On nights that Harold came home with the company van he parked it inside the garage. There was always something too valuable in the van to leave it out overnight. And Harold was a careful man. Harold had kept the vending machine tech job maybe a little longer than a person ought to, so the family could give Sabrina the chance to follow her heart, and her obvious customer skills and business savvy into the yarn store knitting niche. Harold's job, never glamorous but mostly steady, brought benefits and a regular pay check the family could try to build upon. Harold had a solid relationship with the vending business owners who were very hands-on at the warehouse and the office. Working so closely with the owners, Harold was the "on-call" half of the business, but it meant that promotion wasn't possible as long as the owners stayed healthy. So long as Covid didn't trip them, steady just might win the race.

Elsbeth had already written a very readable, kindergartner 'milk' on the grocery list. Sabrina wrapped Elsbeth's blonde hair into a temporary ponytail and leaned over to kiss the top of her daughter's head. "Add pancake mix," she advised Elsbeth. "I've got to get dressed." She didn't ask Elsbeth if she knew how to spell 'pancake', or 'mix'.

Sabrina had only the vaguest of childhood memories of her own mother. The brightest of them all, was of her mother, in their kitchen, in the middle of their everyday morning rush, getting everyone fed and out the door making time to drill Sabrina on her letters and her spelling. All the while getting herself ready to go to work leading the day shift on the milling floor. Sabrina's other vivid memory of her mother was her mother making a fabric stash market for quilters in the neighborhood out of savings and bolt ends from the mill. Sabrina knew exactly

5

where her interest in threads and yarns and colors was born. The direct line between how the young Sabrina grew up and pursued life rock-steady, while moving forward and her mother's own drive and ambition would be a psychologist's field-day. If she had the time. Sabrina wondered what her mother would be like now. She wondered whether she would approve of Sabrina riding both rails -- having a family and running a small business. She and Harold were good together and he was so good with the kids. She wondered whether she had grown to be strong and brave because her mother wasn't there. Or, because the mother Sabrina saw so briefly was only ever brave and strong in her child's eyes. Would the Sabrina she had come to know have grown into the same Sabrina had her mother been there all along? But she didn't have the time to tease through the wonderings.

Sabrina pulled on a pair of navy blue twill slacks before remembering it was missing a vital button at the waist. Folding the slacks carefully, she placed them on her pillow to remind her to do the mending, and then made a quick tug on the bed covers to give them some semblance to a carefully made bed. She chose a pair of brown slacks, one of her favorites because it had so many pockets. She matched the slacks with a tan turtleneck, and another of her favorites, a knit Azteca vest. Which had been a lot of work. In bright colors, silky, soft and smooth, handspun, hand-dyed, 100% virgin alpaca yarn. So happy it could push out the fears and apprehensions, for a while.

Back in the kitchen she asked Elsbeth, "Do you know what you are going to wear today? You better run and get dressed. We need to be leaving pretty soon." She removed the last cold waffle from the waffle iron and began nibbling on the edges. She emptied the dishwasher and reloaded it with the breakfast dishes.

Elsbeth bounced back into the kitchen like a bright-hued sprite. Sabrina had knitted her sweater too. Sabrina was always knitting – when the business and the family weren't on the front burner. Knitting was as easy and natural for her as whistling is for other people. And because it was so natural, she could knit while multitasking on anything that didn't require hands-on. And, because she always had knitting at hand, she could feel good about filling any 'gap-time' that fell into her day. Sabrina knew that might be what most knitters, crocheters, and cross-stitchers loved about their 'hobby'. "Don't you look nice," she told her daughter as she motioned for Elsbeth to follow her through the screened side porch to the driveway. "Got your face mask?" Looking at her mobile phone, Sabrina decided she had time to drive a few extra miles to her favorite grocery store.

The grocery store, known as McKeever's Fine Foods, was owned by the McKeevers for a very long time. It occupied space in a new building in an old neighborhood called, "The Green".

Another favorite store in the next block was an old-fashioned hardware store where Anna, Harold's mother, otherwise known to the children as Nana, liked to shop. They had one of everything. Stores seemed to come and go. One would be replaced by something else, like a movie theater was now an antique store. The old City Hall had been turned over to a Historical Society for the county's Early Days Museum. City Hall was undergoing a change of exhibits to include the stories from more peoples who had lived in the area over a much longer span of time. The Caribbean Deli, where Sabrina had occasionally stopped, had a big hand-drawn sign in the front window: "WE'RE MOVING! Follow US!". Hastily pulling into a parking place she could read the smaller printing that gave the Deli's new address on Huron street. Even better – Sabrina's yarn shop was on Huron. She wasn't able to read the new address without getting out of the car, but she suspected it was probably the space that until recently had been home to a candle shop.

Sabrina was pleased to find the McKeevers parking lot relatively empty. Even more pleased to see that her friend, Laurin McCurnin, had followed her into the parking lot. "Put your face mask on," she told Elsbeth, and led her over to Laurin's car.

Laurin, pulling a face mask from her jacket pocket, greeted Sabrina with a weak smile. Talking across a distance of six feet they advanced toward the grocery store. Other times they might have agreed to stop at the store's coffee counter and enjoyed a cup of coffee, but today neither one of them made the suggestion. They had first met a long time ago when Sabrina's son, Nathan, and Laurin's son, Patrick, were preschoolers. Sabrina thought Laurin was thinner, her dress was hanging a little loosely from her shoulders, and she had a swollen appearance around both eyes.

"How are things going these days?" said Laurin.

"The shop isn't setting any records. I'm thinking of trying to develop more online business, especially if Harold has time to help me," said Sabrina straightening her mask.

"Harold is working from home?" inquired Laurin.

"No, he can't repair vending machines from home. A lot of the offices are shut down and most employees are working from home so there aren't as many vending machine service-calls, either. Harold gets all the calls because the other two guys have been furloughed. Things have really slowed down. How is your family surviving?" Sabrina asked politely.

"Being a cop, Irwin can't work from home either. The city has furloughed a lot of employees, but if anything the police force is understaffed. I hope this defund-the-police movement doesn't gain any ground. I'm probably going to close the dress shop permanently. I can't afford to order more inventory. Of course, we're doing no business in alterations either. The landlord is offering me a break because he doesn't want to see any more empty spaces in the Centerville neighborhood, but it may not be enough."

"It's too bad garments to clothe the human body isn't an 'essential business'." Sabrina offered.

Laurin's listless voice trailed almost to a whisper. "My grandfather's in a nursing home and none of us have been allowed to see him for several months. Every time we take groceries to my grandmother she cries about it. She's afraid he's going to die alone. She's afraid she may die alone." She stopped before naming any more of her fears.

Sabrina and Laurin had so much in common. Children at the same ages, putting everything on the line for their small businesses. And now Covid. Laurin's eyes glistened. "So many in the nursing home have already died. How's Harold's mother, Anna?"

"She stays healthy by staying at home, she calls it being cloistered instead of quarantine. At least she keeps her sense of humor," Sabrina said with a little smile before continuing. "Harold gets her groceries, no outside contacts except for the kids. She has them on days they aren't in-person at school, but if they get exposed, they could infect her before we know it. I know how lucky we are to have Harold's mother so involved with the kids."

"Laurin, look at that!" Sabrina pointed to the signage on the doors. "The grocery store has every glass panel covered with MASKS REQUIRED posters. That might be a little overkill."

Laurin eased her way toward the doors. "I'd better get moving. I need cereal for the boys and I've got my grandmother's grocery list."

Sabrina followed Laurin inside, waiting while Laurin pulled two sanitizing wipes from a waist-high dispenser. She nodded at Elsbeth to retrieve a sanitizing wipe for their cart. The wipes did not separate neatly and Elsbeth had more than she needed to wipe down the handles of the shopping cart. Elsbeth, while riding on the front-end of the card, held the shopping list while Sabrina tried to recall other things they might need.

"Mom, I put ice cream on the list. Can we get some ice cream?" Elsbeth asked.

"Yes. One vanilla and one of your choice, but we'll not get those until we have all the other things. They might have some fresh cranberries at the far end of the produce section."

Sabrina raised her head in alarm when she heard shouting at the front of the store. Sabrina grabbed Elsbeth's hand, and made her way silently up one of the aisles. Astounded, she was sure she was hearing Laurin's voice.

A deep male voice came close to overpowering both Laurin and another female. "Sir," said the other female, "it's clearly posted –"

"Damn your posters. It's all a hoax of the left-wing liberals and the fake news promoters. The truth is it's no worse than the flu that we have every winter. People die. People always die. And we gotta live. I gotta work to feed my kids, pay the rent . . ."

"You no-maskers are the ones super-charging the spread," Laurin practically shrieked. "You're killing my grandfather. You obviously don't care anything about other people, at least you ought to care about yourself. Have some pride. Have some shame." She was crying hard now, but standing straight, and tall, and glaring at the maskless oaf.

Sabrina had inched her way close enough to the front to see a huge, tall bearded man, clad in several layers of flannel and heavy corduroy waving his arms threateningly as he broadcast his opinion.

"It's my constitutional right to not wear a mask – it's a free decision–"

"You don't care if I lose my business," Laurin accused, her face crimson with anger.

Sabrina glanced at Elsbeth. It would be hard to get Elsbeth clear of the mayhem if things got out of hand. As she thought of retreating to the back of the store in search of an exit, she caught sight of a row of shopping carts being shoved inside the store through a five-foot-high opening in the side wall. Sabrina and Elsbeth hurriedly exited through the opening. Sabrina hoped her friend wouldn't turn to see her take the side exit instead of joining her defense. Bending over and pulling in her stomach Sabrina squeezed past the carts toward the parking lot through the opening, but caught her knit vest by a few yarns. She jerked the vest free.

"We didn't get the ice cream," came Elsbeth's shrill protest. Elsbeth should have gotten through more easily, but she bumped her head sharply on the frame of the opening. And out they went. Quickly. Safe in her car, Sabrina couldn't stop trembling. She was catching her breath, hoping she hadn't scared Elsbeth with their unconventional exit.

"Let me look at your head," she told her daughter, but her hands were shaking so bad, she could hardly brush Elsbeth's hair away from her scalp.

Sabrina's internal voice called her a coward! She was a coward. She should have stepped up to Laurin's side and joined her in the torrid argument. Coward! She bent Elsbeth's head over and could see a lump starting to develop, but at least no blood. She was a coward and had lost a friend. No matter whether Laurin had seen her shameful departure or not. No matter how it ended, Laurin knew Sabrina was in the store somewhere. The swelling on Elsbeth's head could be helped with a stop for a sweet treat somewhere, the torn vest could be repaired, but she would never again have an opportunity to come to Laurin's defense. Coward!

HAROLD

Chapter Two

N ana says you're not very attentive to your laptop lessons."

Harold heard no response from his son in the van's passenger seat, which proved to him that Nana was right.

"It wouldn't surprise me if she didn't take your phone away from you. Hold it hostage until your lessons are done." In fact, Harold had already suggested that exact move to Nana and Sabrina both. He had, more than once, remarked to Sabrina that they were very lucky to have an available grandmother to help with the children through this horrible nightmare. He had actually made a point of thanking his mother for her help in front of Sabrina. Most of his peers didn't have a standby babysitter.

A sharp, static-laden voice interrupted their one-sided conversation. "Any of you going south on the Strawn OverPass? You need to look for an alternate route. Emergency vehicles coming from both directions. This is WBØYGHB."

"WBØYGHB, this is CK2RRLV. Have you heard Stan this morning?"

"CK2RRLV, this is WBØYGHB. Stan was on earlier. I heard him about 6:15."

"Thanks, I want to ask him something about coax – can you get that at the candy store? CK2RRLV, the name is Mike. Back to you, WBØYGHB."

"That's a roger. I'm sure you can. Strawn OverPass has turned into a parking lot. I'm going to be late at my destination. WBØY-GHB."

"CK2RRLV. I'm about destinated, too. Catch you down the line. This is CK2RRLV. 73. Over and out."

Harold kept silent for a few minutes waiting to see if anyone else came on frequency. No one else called. Harold was hooked on amateur radio. Amateur radio was friends and fascination. It was intricate and technical. It was his safe and meaningful connection to a world outside his job and his family. He was glad that Sabrina tolerated his preoccupation and hoped that some time it would click with her and she would get a ham license, too; lots of ham wives also held licenses. Funny, but sometimes you would hear spousal pairs talking to each other on a net as if they didn't even know each other. Harold wondered how they talked to each other at home.

He had given the current amateur radio technician's license manual to Nathan, but he was hesitant about asking Nathan if he had spent any time looking at it. A lot of the long-time hams had gotten their first license when they were in their mid-teens. Back then learning Morse Code had been a requirement. Dah dit dah dit dah dah dit dah! All of the older hams knew the code, even if they hadn't used it for years. The Code had become a suggestion. Harold knew one long-time ham who claimed his dreams were in Morse Code.

What Harold heard next brought both pleasure and dismay.

"Isn't that a new hand-held?" Nathan asked.

He was pleased that Nathan had recognized the new hand-held transceiver, although its appearance was not that different from the others. The dismay came because he had not yet mentioned the expensive purchase to Sabrina. Thank heavens they had the yarn shop income. If he got a cut-down in hours, or even laid off, they might still have money to survive.

Harold opened his mouth, but said nothing. How could he compliment his son on recognizing a new piece of equipment and ask him not to mention it to his mother. And even if he asked him, the tidbit of information might slip out inadvertently.

"Don't upset Nana. She still misses Grandpa."

"I know." Nathan's tone was teenager strained.

Harold turned for a searching look at his son.

"When is Nana going to die?" Nathan asked, his voice lowered.

"Not for a long time, we hope."

"When is this . . . thing . . . going to be over?" Nathan's words were stronger but his brow was furrowed.

"That's what not even the experts can tell."

They rode in silence for a bit.

"Dad, what's a hoax?"

"It's like . . . when somebody tries to play a trick on you. Why do you ask?"

"Alford's uncle says all this crazy stuff about people getting sick, it's all just a hoax and taking away people's constitutional rights."

"Nathan, do you know what the Constitution is?"

"It's something a bunch of old guys wrote a long time ago."

"Have you ever heard it called the 'law of the land'?"

"Yeah."

"Its a big promise that all the people make to each other, so that they agree to try to protect everyone's rights, even when they don't agree."

"It just sounds complicated."

"It is complicated . . ."

Harold swung into the driveway of Nana's house. " . . ask Nana. She can explain." Harold knew that his mother had a way of explaining complicated things in a way that even children could understand. While he adjusted his mask around his ears, he looked at the condition of the siding. The house was going to need a fresh coat of paint before long. If Nana hadn't moved into something smaller by then. Or into an assisted living facility. Nana, or Anna Harkins to her neighbors and friends, had been a godsend to help with the children. The transition from Anna to Nana had come breezily and naturally to her as the grandchildren had come along She was still young, relatively, and healthy, but once the Pandemic was over it would be good for her to be where care could be provided for her if needed. The house would still need to be painted to get it ready for the market. As they made their way along the sidewalk to the door, Harold grabbed Nathan for a hug around his shoulders. "Let's make this a good day."

In anticipation of their arrival, the door was unlocked. Nathan headed across the kitchen to a sunlit window bench on the far side of the dining room and was immediately engrossed in one of his games on his phone. Petunia, the sweetest of Nana's two cats, jumped up on the bench and rubbed against Nathan's leg.

"Are Dad's C-clamps still in the garage?" Harold asked Nana as she came into the kitchen. Harold motioned with his head for her to follow him toward his father's workbench. It wasn't until his father became ill that Harold realized how much help his father had been with home maintenance, with himself as a willing co-worker. Harold had come to realize, too, that the time spent working hand tools with his father's sometimes not too patient guidance was the very set of skills that had helped him earn and keep a career. Now that his father was gone, Harold acknowledged that the maintenance for two homes fell squarely on his shoulders. Nathan was willing enough as a helper, but at twelve, lacked the physical strength for most jobs. Harold knew that he needed to spend more time with Nathan – just as his father had patiently planted the skill to not be afraid of hard work, and hand-work. When Nana was at the middle of the two steps down to the garage level, he shut the door behind her.

"You told Sabrina that Nathan wasn't doing a good job with his online lessons?"

"Yes. Well, in a way I don't blame him. He gets linked up okay, but then he has to wait for someone else to come online. There are too many gaps. And then he has his phone, under the table, texting to his friends. Too bad there isn't a career called Multi-Tasking. We're training a generation of 'em." From her position on the middle step Nana could talk to her son eye-to-eye.

"We talked a little about that. Why don't you make him put the phone on the table until the lessons are done?" Remembering that they had told Nana she couldn't go to the hair salon, he noted that she was fastening her grey hair into a bun. With a bright scarlet ribbon.

"Good idea. I'll try that." It wasn't sarcasm.

"Otherwise, how do you think he's getting along?"

"About as well as any other 12-year-old living in a new world he doesn't understand. Why do you ask?"

"On the way over he was asking me about what a hoax was." He was also asking me when his grandmother was going to die – his pert, youngish grandmother with scarlet ribbons in her hair.

"Oh, Alford. That's one of his texting buddies. I don't think they are in the same class. I am pretty sure I don't like Alford. At least I don't trust him."

"Try to discourage the connection if you can."

Coming back into the kitchen, Nana made headway for the counter next to the refrigerator; she cupped both hands around the edge of a pie that had mysteriously appeared on her kitchen counter.

"What's that?" Harold asked.

"Nothing," Nana said quickly.

Nathan, all his attention focused on the phone in his hands, seemed not to have moved from his place on the window bench.

"I'm leaving, son," Harold called He would try to remember later to ask Nathan how the pie had so magically appeared. One thing he knew he couldn't ask Nathan was why Nana had been so curt in her response.

Ham net chatter filled the van as Harold drove on to work after dropping Nathan at Nana's. As he entered the vending company parking lot, he could see some stepped-up activity loading the company delivery truck at the shipping dock. Harold waved at the guys as he turned toward the front office. His boss, Arney Faulkner, was waiting for him at the front door. Harold had known Arney long enough to know he was smiling under his mask. "I've got some good news – for a change." He led Harold to the office. "Overlake Hospital has ordered four more vending machines. They're doing a hand-over-fist business. Damned Covid. At least somebody's busy."

Irene Faulkner, who ran the small business's books quite capably, scolded her husband "I don't feel all that good making our hay off of someone else's bad luck. I don't want them any busier than they need to be. Just saying." Harold could tell they had talked about this before. He was hearing a shared bit of marriedspeak. Arney continued, "I called a couple of the guys to help with delivery. The first two machines have already been delivered, waiting for you to do the installation. The other two are on the way." Arney was busy writing as he talked, and finished with shoving two pieces of paper across his desk to Harold. Irene came closer, looked them over, and smiled at Harold.

Harold found himself actually smiling too, something he rarely had done in recent weeks. Installing new vending machines was a heck of a lot easier than repairing machines that had quit functioning. The machines often took a lot of abuse. Harold was old enough to remember all of the slugs and fake coins people used to try to slip into the vending machines. More recently, he had pulled photocopied dollar bills out of the paper changers. People still try to bully the machines for a bag of chips from time to time. Harold found himself a chuckle: but the machines don't care, they do their job and don't give in to bullies.

Arney tapped on one of the sheets. "This is a new location. Waiting room in pediatric section."

"I can find it." Unfortunately, Harold remembered the pediatric ward very well, from the time that Elsbeth had scared the wits out of all of them with some breathing problems. That was a tough night.

Harold had been aware of on-going new construction at the

hospital. As he approached the entry driveways, he could see that the covered parking area had been cordoned off.

Harold knocked on an unmarked maintenance department door and was met with a shout. "We can't let you in here – you have to come in through the E.R." Harold thought he recognized the voice. "Vince, is that you?"

"Yeah. Sorry I can't let you in. They'll take your temperature at the E.R. I'll meet you in pediatrics."

The delivery crew had left the vending machines exactly where they needed to be. Harold set his canvas tool bag against the wall. His friend Vince arrived full speed, pushing rolling shelves loaded with boxes and packets of various foods. Vince wore a face mask with a Dallas Cowboys logo. Vince Garretson, who had become VP Facilities at Overlake Hospital, was always moving at full speed. That's likely why he got the job managing the hospital complex in the first place. Certainly it was what was keeping the job for him.

"Ah, good," came a female voice. "We've been close to starving up here." The way she said it there was more than one 'a' in sta-arving.

Harold had not seen his former high school classmate, Candace Phipps, for some time, but he knew she worked at the hospital as a psychologist or psychiatrist or some kind of head doctor. Candace wore a pediatric smock under a transparent plastic coverall garment that fastened in the back. Her face mask was a print with children in swings. Harold shifted his feet to stand face to face. "Hospital all filled up, is it?"

"And then some. We're all working long hours. Don't get sick – we may not have any room for you."

Candace had started to walk away, but she turned back and faced Harold again. "You have a couple of kids, don't you?"

"Yes," he nodded, wondering why Candace had asked.

She hesitated, then asked: "How are they taking the Pandemic?"

Harold paused as well. "Okay, I guess." Why had Nathan wanted to talk about a hoax? "They don't have any adult memories to compare."

She turned again to move on. Then said: "Just pay close attention to them. We're experiencing here in the hospital some children who are having trouble processing things. They're worried without knowing what to be worried about. Or how."

"Thanks for the heads-up."

NANA

Chapter Three

The minute the door closed on Harold, Nana turned toward her grandson. "I presume it was Daylor Carruthers who brought the pie?"

She nodded at the house on the other side of two, side-by-side, driveways.

Without taking his eyes off his phone, Nathan gave an affirmative nod.

"Do you like pumpkin pie?"

This time Nathan's reply was a negative shake.

"Good. All the more for me," his grandmother said sharply.

Nathan's head turned, his eyes widened with surprise.

"The next time Daylor Carruthers comes to the door, please let me know."

Nathan continued his stare.

"What did I just say?"

"To come get you when someone comes to the door."

"Good. I hope you remember that." She looked at the Delft clock on the wall over the stove. "You have about fifteen minutes before class begins. Are you hungry or did you eat at home?"

"At home."

Nana grabbed her land-line phone on the second ring. The caller ID showed the number of the Pleasant Valley nursing home. She hadn't talked to her friend, Marjorie Dannefort, for several days.

"Margie?"

"Thank heavens you're home. I was afraid you would be out."

"Where would I go? I'm hunkered down at home."

"They let the telephone people in the building late yesterday afternoon. They got the phones working again – for the meantime. No telling how long before the phones go out again."

Trying to move her friend away from what must certainly be the dreary daily details of living in a care facility, Anna said: "I'm so glad you could call. How's everything?"

"I think three more have died. The nursing staff is so busy and so worn out they won't tell us anything, and you can't believe the custodial people, they'll say anything."

"You still confined to your room?"

"Absolutely. I feel like such a prisoner. I'm living in an old French novel," explained Marjorie. "They've actually moved some of the doubles into the empty rooms. Our population is rapidly thinning out, and we don't see some of the custodial people anymore. The only answer we get is that they can't come because they are in quarantine." Marjorie's voice faltered, and softened. Nana could hear the catch in her friend's throat. "I think Mr. Deakins died yesterday."

Nana felt her heart twinge. "He was your . . . special friend, wasn't he?"

Marjorie's response was delayed. "No one will confirm that for me. I tried to sneak out in the hall to get to his room, but one of the nurses walked me back. I would have tried to call his son, but the phones weren't working. The son doesn't know me, but the last time Mr. Deakins and I talked he gave me the son's name and phone number. His son lives in Arizona. I'll probably call him later in the morning."

"So sorry to hear that."

"What have you been doing these days? Seems like we haven't

talked in years."

Nana laughed. "My hair's about gotten long enough for a pony tail. Sally's is open for business – I guess they're considered essential – but Harold won't let me go."

"They were letting a barber in here on a limited basis. Mr. Deakins got a haircut a week ago. He had gotten rather shaggy. I asked him if he was 'going hippy' on me." Anna could almost hear a slight smile. Marjorie continued, "Are your grandkids back in school?"

"Sort of. They're both on a crazy schedule. In school one day – online the next. The school calls it hybrid. Most days I have one of them here at the house with me. Sometimes both. But they get along fine. Harold has to go to work – you can't repair vending machines at home. And Sabrina is trying to keep the yarn shop in business, despite lockdown orders that seem to keep changing. She had one customer who needed just one more skein to finish an Einstein coat, so she sent that one in the mail."

"I wish I had some knitting. I'm going stir-crazy here."

"What would you like? I could bring you a kit. Take a look at Sabrina's website. There's lots of interesting stuff."

"That's a good idea. I better hang up. Custodial is here and they want me out of the way."

"Okay. Call when you can. Go on-line. Let me know if I can get you something."

"That would be nice. Quiet knitting sitting can be a comfort," said Marjorie. Then quickly added, "Check the obituaries for me, if you get a chance. See if you find Mr. Deakins' name. Bye –" The conversation ended abruptly. Maybe Marjorie was distracted, thought Nana. Marjorie was always so polite. People were just a little more brusque with this Covid around.

Nana was pleased to see that Nathan was at the dining room table and had opened his laptop.

She decided not to confiscate his mobile phone; instead she pulled the head chair around to the side and sat down with her knitting. She would be able to see his screen and whether or not he had a hand on his phone under the table.

As soon as she settled, both cats came to twine themselves around her legs. Petunia and Pansy, from the same mother but not the same litter, they looked so much alike – brown and white and caramel – that few people tried to distinguish which was which. But Petunia was just the tiniest bit bigger. Anna was trying to work out a pattern that would create a knit pumpkin sofa pillow. Lord knows there aren't enough knit pumpkin sofa pillows, she thought, and smiled. It was a challenge. So far she had frogged it out two times already and it looked like she was headed for a third. Together, she and Sabrina had created the Chameleon Scarf, a happy discovery for which Sabrina had written the instructions and entered in a yarn company competition. Their winning entry had become the yarn company's property and had helped sell countless meters of the company's yarns. She planned to alert Sabrina about the pumpkin project – maybe they could be winners again working together.

From what Nana could see, Nathan was working on some math problems, algebra she guessed. She'd been good at algebra in high school, but everything was different now.

She remembered back when Harold was in middle school and even Hank, as they called Harold Sr., who ran the City of Overlake Water Department, hadn't been able to help his son with the 'new math'."

She missed Hank Sr.. Terribly. After he died, even before the Pandemic, it had gotten more difficult to talk to Harold and Sabrina about him. Nathan and Elsbeth would ask about Grandpa from time to time. They all missed Hank, too, in their own way. Their conversations with Nana concerning Hank were always short, and sometimes it seemed to Nana that they weren't even talking about the same subject. Now, after the Pandemic made its terrible presence known, conversations with Harold and Sabrina became lectures, don't go anywhere, don't leave the house, you don't need a mask because we don't want you to go anywhere anyway, and don't let anyone in the house. They worried about her. They worried about the children too. She sensed some of their deeper fears.

Sabrina was also afraid the yarn shop would fail, but she was relieved that they could count on Harold's' income. The vending machine business had dropped so low Harold half expected to be furloughed any day but he was encouraged by how doggedly Sabrina pursued the yarn shop's income streams. Nana wavered between thinking she should encourage them to share their anxieties and other times believing they would have better mental health if they remained ignorant of each other's vague fears. The looming future was approaching fast enough on its own without any encouragement from Nana.

The house was so quiet Nana jumped at a knock on the side door. It was her neighbor, Daylor Carruthers, the black Covid mask on his face could not hide the frown on his forehead. He held a single sheet of paper in his hand.

Nana pulled the door open, but left the glass-paneled storm door closed. The Carruthers and the Harkins had been good neighbors for many years, but now that Emmie Carruthers had passed away and Hank Harkins was gone, Nana was uncertain about her relationship with Daylor. Sometimes they were the same close neighbors they had been before, and other times it seemed that he was wooing her. And she was totally indecisive as to whether she liked it or not. Sometimes she felt like a high school girl hoping for an invitation to the prom.

Daylor, Dayl to his friends, was waving the sheet of paper up and down. "It's from my granddaughter, Tressa," he said. "I just got it. I printed it out. I need to ask you about it."

Nana nodded and went back to the kitchen coat rack for her denim barncoat. As she closed the door her fingers snagged the pink bandanna that was hanging on the door knob. Harold and Sabrina had implied that since she was not leaving her home she didn't need a mask, but they couldn't keep people from coming to her door.

Bright bandanna tied on to cover her nose and mouth, Nana pushed open the storm door. Surprised, Dayl stepped nimbly to the side.

"Nathan is here with me today," Nana explained. "He's doing

his online school work. We can talk on the porch." She sat in the wooden rocker closest to the door and motioned to the other rocker. "Move that one over here." If they sat side to side as they talked they would not be spewing atomized whatever on each other. They certainly weren't close enough for that. She sat down and waited for Dayl.

With one hand Dayl positioned the rocker. He kept shaking the piece of paper, but did not offer it to her to be read. "Anna," he began. "Anna, I don't know what to do." His voice drooped with despair.

"Well, Dayl, there's no way I can help you if I don't know what's upsetting you." She made a half-gesture to take the paper from his hand. She noted that what remained of Dayl's hair was turning grey, maybe even more grey than hers. Hank, with a full head of hair until the day he died, was the envy of some of his friends

"It's Teresa Mae. Tressa. They're closing down her college and she wants to come here."

Nana made a decisive move and took the paper from Dayl's hand. In the e-mail Tressa had explained that she didn't want to go home because both her parents were ill with Covid-19, and they were afraid Tressa's younger siblings would catch the virus as well. Tressa's request seemed to Nana like a very reasonable solution to the problem. "I presume Tressa would be able to continue her classes online?" Just like Nathan. In fact, hopefully, she might be a good role model for Nathan.

"I'm just not used to having a young person around all the time."

"Dayl, Tressa used to visit you all the time when Emmie was still here."

"That's just it. Tressa and Emmie were able to talk about . . . women things . . ."

"I'm always next door."

Dayl seemed not to have heard. " . . . like boyfriends and dating . . . and music!"

Nana thought about how hard it must be to be a college student with no social life without death defying risk. Covid was changing everything. Maybe the most likely to make it through the Covid era would be younger people. It might seem just a passing season to them.

Dayl was still talking. "... Emmie had her quilt stuff out. The sewing machine was going all the time ..."

"With the quilting I'm no help, but I could teach her how to knit. I think you should tell her that she is quite welcome. Would do you good to have a young person around."

"I'm kind of getting set in my ways."

"Tressa could probably help you with some of your computer issues. I haven't been checking on you but 'your ways' could probably do with a little feminine ironing out too. Having her around a while would be good for you."

Dayl relaxed a bit and settled back into the rocker. Nana heard him take a big, calming breath. She could see him seem to reach some conclusion. And then, refocusing on her, he asked: "How are things going in your world, Anna?"

Nana handed the paper back to Dayl. "I keep wondering what normal is now. I usually have one of Harold's children here with me, but rarely both of them on the same day. The world seems so different."

"Your son and his wife ... Sabrina?"

Nana sighed. "They're so busy trying to figure out what to do I don't think they ever talk to each other." She reflected for a moment – should she share her concerns with Dayl? That would be like ... family.

Why not – he had brought his troubles to her – she ventured: "Harold's afraid he will be furloughed and they'll be dependent on the income from Sabrina's shop, and Sabrina is afraid she'll be forced to close the shop and they'll be living on Harold's paycheck. And they don't talk to each other about it. I don't know how to get them to share their worries."

"Maybe it's better that they don't."

They both sat in thought for a minute or two. The simple comfort of knowing company. Nana broke the quiet.

"I haven't cut into that pumpkin pie I know you snuck into my kitchen," she looked at him square on, "but I know it will be delicious." If she didn't have Nathan in the house she might ask Dayl to come and share lunch. They could sit at both ends of the dining room table, be the required six feet apart, and still carry on a decent conversation.

"If Tressa were here she could help me with the cooking." Dayl stood up. "Maybe I'll send Tressa a reply. I'll tell her you have a pair of needles and some yarn waiting for her."

Nana hung her barncoat back on the clothes rack and left the pink bandanna dangling from the door knob.

"Nana?" Nathan called from the dining room. "You had a call from Mr. Windle. He said he had found a house for you. Wants you to call him back. I wrote down his number."

Smiling despite her irritation, Nana took the piece of paper with the telephone number. When she called Mr. Windle back, sometime after Harold had picked up Nathan, she'd give him an earful – in the future, should he call her number again, he was to speak to no one except her. No one in the family knew that she had been looking for a smaller home. What should she say to Nathan? Ask him to keep quiet? Or keep quiet herself and pretend that Mr. Windle did not exist. A sudden thought shot through her mind. She frowned at the piece of paper. "I don't know any Mr. Windle. He must have gotten the wrong number."

"He asked for you – Mrs. Harkins."

"There is more than one family named Harkins." She looked over Nathan's shoulder. He was no longer connected to a math class. From the wordage – although she was too far away to read specific things – he must have shifted to an English class, or maybe history.

Nathan noticed his grandmother's attention to his computer screen. "Somebody in England thinks they have discovered the correct location for the battle of Hastings in 1066."

Nana leaned over to look at the laptop. "My coffee got cold while I was talking to Mr. Carruthers. Do you want something to drink?"

27

Nathan gave her a negative shake and returned to his computer screen. "King Harold was defeated. King Harold. Is that how my grandfather got his name?"

"No. That was a long time ago." She smiled, "How old do you think your grandfather was?" The phone sounded again, but Nana carried her mug of cold coffee with her to pick up the phone back in the kitchen. Her friend, Marjorie Dannefort, again. What could have happened now?

"Anna!" Marjorie's voice was excited. "The best news. Mr. Deakins is still alive – they moved him to a different room. I think he is okay."

"That is exciting. How'd you find out?"

"One of the aides who brought me my lunch. She didn't know much but she knew where he is. When they get down to the skeleton night staff I'm going to go see if I can find him. I'm so happy."

NATHAN

Chapter Four

F riday morning Nathan was more than ready for an in-person day at school.

It was a new school for him, a newly-built building, finished in spite of the Pandemic, open mid-year, a middle school for seventh to ninth graders. Nathan was just beginning to find his way around when the school administration had switched to a hybrid form of conducting lessons switching between online classrooms and in-person attendance. Nathan had barely had enough time to recognize old classmates from grade school, and begin to get acquainted with new fellow students. It would be nice if he could get there a little early, but his father dawdled over his morning coffee. He always seemed to on Fridays. His father was putting on a blustery alls-okay attitude.

"I'm going to make one of those plexiglass-panel protectors for the shop this afternoon." Harold told Sabrina. "Nathan and I might be able to install it late this afternoon. Elsbeth going to spend the day with Nana?"

"Yes. We're going to check out some books from the library. They'll do a curbside delivery and we can pick them up on the way to Nana's."

"I better be sure I still have the right kind of mouldings I'll need. We'll get to work on it as soon as I pick Nathan up from school." He stood up abruptly. "Let's move, buddy." He picked up his handi-talky from the center of the table.

Nathan had already opened the van door when Sabrina summoned Harold back to the kitchen door. She motioned Harold inside. Nathan could hear only a bit of the whispered conversation but at the words 'it's a big birthday, he'll be a teen-ager' he knew they were talking about his birthday. He was all the way into the van and had the door shut by the time his father reappeared.

Ominously there were very few cars in the middle school parking lot. "Are you sure it's an in-school day for you?" Harold asked.

"Yeah. But it's still a little bit early," Nathan said, although it wasn't. "They'll all be rolling in." He opened the door.

"I'm going to watch until I see you get inside. Pull your mask up."

It seemed strange, even to Nathan, that there was no one in view. Striding up to the entry doors, Nathan told himself to be prepared to find the doors locked. To his amazement, the door opened readily. He turned to wave a good-bye to his father.

Through the second set of doors was a huge, darkened space that served as a part-assembly hall and part-cafeteria. With no lights on, it was difficult to see the other side of the immense room. He was unwilling yet to admit he had made a mistake in reading the calendar. Glancing back through the entryway he could see the tail-lights of the van swing out of the school driveway onto the wider street.

Okay, he thought, let's explore the school. He pulled his mask down around his neck. The school offices were to the right of the entryway. All four doors to various sections of the office were locked. Nathan moved on down the hallway to the boys' restroom. There was no door, the entryway was a double baffle. Two high windows provided a little light. His pee hitting the urinal was the only sound in the eerie morning quiet. Maybe.

Nathan froze as he thought he sensed someone else in the building. He made a quick dodge for the side stall where he could close the door. Cautious, he climbed up on the toilet seat so that someone peering under the door would not be able to see his feet. Yes, there definitely was someone else inside the building who had come into the boys' restroom to use the urinal. Being careful not to show his fingers clutching to the top of the wall, Nathan looked over the top of the stall wall.

Alford!

He was looking at the top of Alford's head! Unbelievable that the other person in the building was Alford. It was like radar. Or something. Nathan jumped to the floor and shouted Alford's name before he reached the door.

When Nathan stepped around the stall door, Alford was half-collapsed against the wall – a kid having a heart attack. Alford sagged comically against the wall when he saw it was Nathan.

"What the hell are you doing here?" Alford put his hand on his chest. "Now I know what my grandmother means when she says I've scared the living daylights out of her."

Nathan felt near an apology, but it was hard not to laugh at the same time. "I thought it was an in-school day."

"Naw, it's an at-home day, but I guess my computer broke."

"Why'd you come to school?"

"Just to see if anybody was around. I guess it's just you and me. Bro." Fist bump explosion. Alford was still trying out grownup talking. It was still a little rough.

Together, cool pals, they walked out of the restroom and continued farther down the wide corridor gaining teenage swagger and confidence with every step. They just didn't know it. They tried the doors of each classroom they passed. Nathan was astonished when one of the door knobs gave readily under his hand. As he walked in, Alford was at his heels.

"It's the Spanish classroom," Alford offered. "I was in here on first day. Then I got transferred out."

"How?" Nathan was in a French class and had decided almost from the beginning that he did not like it. It felt like a lifetime commitment.

Alford went straight for the teacher's desk; he jerked open the center drawer. "Want some gum?" He made a fake throw in Nathan's direction.

Nathan made a quick duck. It was one thing to explore – they hadn't broken open any locks – but taking something from a desk would be stealing. Besides, gum chewing was not something he did on a regular basis.

Alford stuffed his mouth with several sticks of gum, and left the wrappings on the middle of the desktop. "My calling card," he explained as if he knew what a calling card really was. Nathan wondered about that.

They explored the somnambulant building, trying every door they found. There was no one there. Nathan vaguely wondered about security, but with no friends to hold them in fun or conversation, and being bound by knowing what would happen if they caused any real damage or mischief, they exited by way of a rear door that locked loudly behind them. Without any plan, Nathan walked alongside Alford. Sooner or later he was going to have to start walking back to school in time for his dad to pick him up. It was easier, for the moment, to follow along with Alford, whom he presumed was going home.

"There won't be anybody at home," Alford offered as advantage. He continued selling. "There might be something we can eat." He suddenly made a dive toward something he spotted on the ground and came up with a dime in his hand. "I found a twenty-dollar bill one time."

"What'd you do with it?"

"My uncle took it away from me."

"Didn't your parents get it back for you?"

"Naw. I got even with him. I took his game box."

They started to cross a boulevard, but stepped back onto the curbing as a police car moved into the outside lane. The policeman behind the wheel gave them a friendly nod of acknowledgment. After the vehicle had finished the turn they started again to cross the boulevard. Alford made a rude gesture and shouted.

"Rebosh the cops."

Nathan stopped on the pavement. "What does that mean?"

"My uncle says that means to take away all their money."

Nathan thought he remembered that his mother knew someone who was related to a policeman. "The uncle who took the twenty-dollar bill away from you?"

"Naw. A different uncle."

"How many uncles do you have?"

"I dunno." Alford led Nathan onto a smaller cross street. "You'll have to meet my grandma. One of my uncles is with her today, cuz his mother had to go to work."

Nathan didn't have time to ask why an uncle had to be with a grandmother because a mother was at work. Maybe the grandmother was so old she needed to have someone sit with her. He had to start walking faster to keep up with Alford. They passed an old beater of a truck with a sticker in the back window of a red, white and blue patriotic symbol on which was imposed the silhouette of a rifle. 'My second amendment rights protect your first amendment rights.' Alford led Nathan onto a driveway and into a one-story ranch-style house. "Looks like grandma's here."

The woman inside didn't look all that elderly, but Alford addressed her as 'Grandma'. Yarn and hook in hand, she was working on a project as she watched the television. Nathan thought he recognized it as a sleeve. In yellow and green. A small boy in a baby walker swung his arms at various bright plastic objects suspended from a framework over his head. A feeding tray in front of the child was empty, but the floor was littered with bits of dry cereal. Two dogs which had been sleeping near a floor furnace duct roused themselves to greet Alford with excited barks and leg brushes. "This is Nathan," Alford explained to his grandmother and the dogs as they passed through the living room on their way to the kitchen.

"Pleased to meet you," Grandma said, never taking her eyes off the television screen. "I see you're one of those maskers. You won't need that here," she said over her shoulder. "We're all healthy as summer hogs."

Involuntarily, Nathan touched the mask still at his neck. Not knowing what to say Nathan muttered a thank-you. Grandma didn't seem to notice. Nathan didn't understand the reference to summer hogs. They were in the heart of a big, metropolitan city; nobody had hogs. Her remark sounded like something that might be said on a farm. Alford had disappeared into the kitchen. Nathan had to compete with the dogs to get through a short hallway.

Alford had pulled the pop-top off a can of beans. He helped himself to two spoons-full directly from the cold can before handing it to Nathan. "Here," he said to Nathan, giving him an extra spoon. From an overhead cabinet he took a loaf of white bread and laid four slices on the bare tabletop. As Alford reached in the refrigerator Nathan could see there was little besides the big bottle of ketchup which Alford removed. Maybe a surprisingly used looking egg carton and an almost empty jug of skim milk. With the same spoon he had used to eat the beans, Alford spread ketchup on two of the bread slices. "Go ahead," he said to Nathan. "Don't you like beans?" He topped both of the slices of bread which held the ketchup with the extra slices and passed one of the sandwiches across the table toward Nathan. With almost the same motion he pulled the can of beans closer to himself for another spoonful.

"I thought you said your uncle was here."

"He is. In there with my grandma."

"There's only a baby in there."

"That's my uncle."

Nathan was silent. Apparently Alford wasn't going to say anything more. Didn't feel the need. Besides, Alford was lost to the ketchup and beans. Nathan took a bite of the ketchup sandwich; it tasted just as weird as he thought it would. He tried to remember what he knew, or had been told, about the spread of Covid-19. By air drafts, which was why people were wearing masks, he thought he remembered, but there was also something about washing hands every hour. Abruptly, Nathan pushed his chair back and made a precipitous plunge for the kitchen sink. He saw nothing that looked like a bar of soap, so he grabbed a bottle of dish-washing liquid.

"What're you doing?" Alford wanted to know.

"Washing my hands. You're supposed to do it every hour." He thought to add: "We've been just about everywhere. Touched just about everything. Covid is . . . "

But Alford wasn't listening. "You believe all that stuff, doncha? It's all just a bunch of moharkey. It's just like the flu. Everybody gets it and then everybody gets over it. That fake news junk is just scare tactics. Haven't you never had the flu?"

"Maybe." Nathan remembered a time he had been so ill he missed a week of school. He looked around for a towel and ended just shaking his hands to shed the moisture. He finished the ketchup sandwich, but left the rest of the beans for Alford.

"Clean up after yourselves," came a command from the living room.

"Yes, ma'am," from Alford. For Alford, cleaning up after himself meant putting the two spoons in the empty bean can and setting it in the sink. "Let's go do some hoops." Alford led Nathan out of the house through a back door. Behind them they heard the grandmother's voice. "You going out, Alford?" Alford didn't bother to answer.

"What time is it?" Nathan took out his mobile phone. "My dad will be coming to pick me up at school. I gotta be starting back." When his mobile phone rang, he could see that the call was from his mother. What was it about mothers that they always seem to know when something isn't right? It was like she knew he wasn't where he was supposed to be and he was holding his phone just now. He froze at the sound of her frightened voice.

"Where are you?" The sound was a tight, throaty monotone.

With no other answer prepared, he blurted the truth. "At Alford's."

His mother swallowed 'Where!#?' and instead asked: "Where does Alford live?"

"On . . . ," he looked at Alford. "What's your address?"

"1609 Garfield."

Nathan repeated for his mother.

"Stay there. Don't go anywhere. Your father is coming to get you. He was at the school and he said there was no one there." Her voice was still high with anxiety.

As Nathan put the mobile phone back in his pocket, Alford threw the basketball at him. Nathan caught the ball and let it drop to the pavement. "My dad's coming to get me." He stopped for another breath. "My mom must be really angry with me."

"What for?"

"Well, I thought it was an in-school day. I didn't tell my dad anything different and let him drop me off. I guess they found out it wasn't an in-school day."

"Parents find out everything," said Alford. Nathan wondered what Alford's 'everything' was. Alford retrieved the ball and carelessly made a throw. "There's one," he shouted as the ball sailed through the hoop. He caught the ball on a bounce and handed it to Nathan.

Nathan made a half-hearted shot which came nowhere near the basket. What would his father say to him when he picked him up? No doubt he would be grounded, but being grounded was not much different from Covid-19 restrictions. Can't go anywhere; can't do anything. He watched Alford make another toss through the hoop; he never seemed to miss. Alford retrieved the ball and threw it to Nathan, who threw it right back. Even if he concentrated on a shot, it was unlikely he would be successful in hitting the hoop. His mind was centered on what his father might say to him.

The van pulled up to the curb. As Nathan opened the door, he looked back at Alford. "See ya," he said. Alford gave him a thumbs up. Nathan shut the door and fastened his seat belt. His father said not a word. They rode twenty minutes to the Harkins home in complete silence.

The house was empty. Nathan assumed his mother was still at the shop; Elsbeth would be with her. In the kitchen, Harold consulted a note Sabrina had left on the refrigerator about meal preparations. Since the yarn shop regular hours were 11 am to 6 pm, Sabrina often was not at home until after 6:30. There had been some days when Nathan had followed his mother's instructions to get the evening meal ready. Today, to Nathan's distress, his father remained silent and didn't look open to any offers of help. Sitting at the table, Nathan tried to imagine what his punishment might be. He was already grounded by the invisible virus. Barring him from watching television, taking away some of his games; even to Nathan those losses seemed insignificant for what he had done. It seemed like nothing wrong at the time. Easy peasy breezy. But he knew it was the wrong thing to do at the end. He hadn't really lied to his parent. It sure felt like it.

Harold broke the silence with a phone call to Sabrina. "Supper's almost ready, how are you doing?" Nathan could hear his mother's voice but could not understand the words.

"About fifteen minutes, then." Harold paused, then said: "Hon, I've got to leave early in the morning to pick up some stuff in Metropole, so you will have to drop Nathan off, if in fact it is an in-school day."

During the entire conversation Harold did not look once in Nathan's direction, as if Nathan were not even in the room.

His father's silence was hurting him more than anything else he could imagine.

SABRINA

Chapter Five

Sabrina was really tired when she locked the door of the shop. She thought she had been on her feet all day.

The shop had not been declared an essential business, and she couldn't let anyone inside, but many of her regular customers had read her message on facebook about curbside delivery. If restaurants were allowed to operate with curbside delivery, why couldn't a yarn shop do the same? She didn't remember how many trips she had made back and forth to get the exact color Mrs. Newquist needed for her needlepoint project. At one point she had thought about rolling the whole display rack out to the curb for Mrs. Newquist to make her selection. She was glad that Mrs. Newquist had ventured out. She needed to check the numbers but it seemed to her like the stay-at-home quarantine world might be causing people to do a little more handwork with their time. Sabrina was not all that excited about making money off of misery but the slight uptick in sales couldn't be coming at a better time.

Elsbeth, ready to throw in and do her part for her Momma, would have been more than willing to carry orders out to the curb, even happy too, but a lot of people did not wear masks when they were in their own cars and Sabrina did not want to risk exposing the child to any more people than necessary. Sabrina knew, without listening to the observations of others that someone could record a negative test, and become infected even before the results came back from the lab. False positive is *not* an oxymoron. Elsbeth kept herself busy tending to the knitted animals in the shop, fluffing them up and sometimes leaving them in a different location. The cat and the dog had a mock spat. Elsbeth kept moving the rabbit, in a vain attempt to keep the ears from flopping over. She rejected all suggestions from her mother to take a nap, but shortly after five collapsed onto the seat of the softest upholstered chair and curled up under an alpacan lap robe. Sabrina had to wake her up a few minutes before closing time.

Sabrina was pleased that she had been able to close at 6. There were several other businesses and offices that closed at the same time and under normal conditions there was a parade of somewhat familiar figures making their way to the distant parts of the parking lots. But conditions were far from normal. Only two people were closing at the same time today and one of them was picked up at the curb. The other person, from the insurance office, Sabrina thought, hastily crossed the street and vanished down the alley. By the time Sabrina reached the alley the figure was gone. But they were not alone. A homeless man – she viewed him as homeless because he appeared to be carrying all his worldly goods on his back – was coming up the alley in her direction. She tightly gripped Elsbeth's hand and thought briefly of changing directions, but that would require them to walk all around the block to reach the car. She quickened her step and gave Elsbeth a tug. As the man passed her she thought he gave her a nod, but she was careful to not be looking at him. Was she seeing more homeless people than before the Pandemic? And homeless people were always causing trouble. The police would have to be more vigilant about protecting property. After she was safely in her car, she dialed Harold on her mobile phone. "I'm leaving the parking lot. Be there soon." As she maneuvered the car the headlights caught another homeless person, huddled in the inset doorway of the downtown hardware store likely turning in for the long night. It would be chilly.

As an essential business the hardware store had been able to stay open, with modifications. They advertised themselves in the newspaper as the hardware store for cooks. Sabrina was still amused about the time, two or three years ago, when she was looking for an immersion blender and an older male clerk, his brow furrowed, told her the store had nothing like that. Fortunately, a woman clerk passed by and immediately interjected, "Oh, yes we do." She even said, "We are the hardware store for cooks." It amused Sabrina then, and amused her now. Odd, how the simplest marketing ideas and the willingness to inventory what the customers were looking for seemed to be a winning small business strategy. Always. And a friendly smile never hurt either. Sabrina thought about what other tried-and-true business stratagems she might be overlooking as she drove home.

For a change, Elsbeth, quite vivacious after her restful nap, had a captive audience at the supper table. "We saw a homeless man in the alley."

Harold's eyebrows shot up in alarm.

"I know he was homeless because his clothes were all dirty."

Harold's head turned to face Sabrina's.

"He was dirty because he doesn't have any place to go to get cleaned up."

Sabrina stared back at Harold, her eyes wary.

"He nodded at Mommy, but she didn't talk to him. We aren't supposed to talk to strangers."

Sabrina jumped in: "Elsbeth, sweetheart, did you have a good time with the animals at the shop today? I could knit you a white bunny so the grey bunny would have someone to play with..."

"There was another homeless man in one of the doorways –"

Sabrina interjected with, "Did you hear what I just said about another bunny?"

Harold's anxious glance turned to his daughter.

40

Elsbeth continued. "Will that man in the doorway sleep there all night?"

"No, sweetheart," Sabrina said softly. "The police will find him and take him to a warming shelter." Sabrina tried to hide her lack of conviction. She had been hearing reports about crowding at the main shelter. Seemed they might be running out of space. And food. And supplies. The Covid toll was everywhere. "Would you go look in the freezer drawer? There might be some frozen cookies on the toppermost shelf," she said to move Elsbeth's attention elsewhere.

Harold and Sabrina spoke only about the meal, with brief mention of what needed to be added to the grocery list. Nathan said not a single word; his mobile phone lay untouched in his lap.

As soon as the dishes were cleared from the table Harold set his laptop at the end farthest from the kitchen. Within ten minutes Sabrina joined her husband with her laptop at the other end, but instead of opening the screen she went to sit where she could look over Harold's shoulder.

"How difficult is it to be a Zoom host?" Sabrina asked.

"Not too bad. It's been a blessing for holding Scout meetings. It's no substitute for being all together at the same place, but it's better than nothing. Why do you ask?"

"Maybe it's a way to get some of the knitters together. That was part of the fun of the store . . . before. Maybe I can figure out some kind of competition. Or a new age knitting circle." That seemed so obvious she was certain that other yarn shops were already testing the conference call waters. Survivors adapt she thought. And move forward. And she didn't want to lose customers. Or friends.

"If you do, I can show you how to manage Zoom. Why don't you watch at the next Scout meeting? You don't have to sign in, just sit here while Nathan and I are on."

Every yarn shop Sabrina had ever been in had a roomy gathering space where customers could sit while knitting. And talking. She thought the gathering area of her store was particularly enticing, two couches facing each other, with individual upholstered chairs, one rocker on either end with a coffee table in the center. Although she didn't like the practice of mixing food with yarn, she did not openly discourage it, and often a knitter would bring homemade delights to share.

Harold was emphatic about being willing to help. "I can help you with something like that, if you want. I don't have to call the net until eight."

"No thanks. Later. Maybe tomorrow. I've been getting a little more action on the Facebook account so I need to pay more attention to getting it updated."

As soon as his mother was seated at her end of the table Nathan brought his laptop and sat down between them.

Shortly before eight o'clock Harold left the room and a few minutes later Sabrina began talking to her son. "Your father says you misinterpreted the in-school schedule and let him drop you off at an empty school. He wondered why you didn't call him when you realized there was no one there." She didn't tell Nathan exactly how Harold said it.

"I didn't want to bother him because he was on his way to work. People were waiting for him at the other end, so I was going to walk home."

"But you didn't. You went to Alford's. Gave me a panic when he called from the school that there was no one there."

"I'm sorry. We just . . . ," he started. But he remembered their talk about 'but' doesn't belong in an apology; you're either sorry or you're not; without excuses. "Can I apologize to him? He won't talk to me. He didn't say anything to me all the way home." Nathan's voice lowered, "Or at supper." It was clear that the distance was hurting Nathan.

"I'll talk with him . . . tonight."

Sabrina studied her son's face. She was puzzled by her husband's behavior, by his silence. Nathan was obviously contrite, and perhaps more confused than she was over Harold's scarcity of words regarding Nathan. In the early years of their parenting, Harold had often demonstrated a short fuse and meted out punishment on the spot. He had slowly forced himself to slow down, regain his temper before determining an appropriate response to childish transgressions. During supper, Sabrina had realized that Harold was studying Nathan for long unguarded moments. Nathan had been very quiet, too, frequently glancing at his father when Harold was not looking at him. Oblivious to the tension, Elsbeth had filled with silence with five year old chatter.

Sabrina called to Elsbeth. "It's going to be your bedtime. If you want a bubble bath you better get in the bathtub now." Sabrina thought she had almost as much pleasure from the bubble baths as Elsbeth and would regret when Elsbeth didn't need her anymore. Elsbeth's sixth birthday was in the next few weeks. Their baby was growing up fast right in front of them. Sabrina was enjoying every bit of it. She hoped Harold was too. Nathan was also growing up. And Sabrina was desperate to make certain not too fast. Today was a near-miss she thought. And the unforgiving calendar had Nathan down for turning into a teenager in just weeks. She was, mostly, ready for Nathan to grow from loved boy-child into a teenager. She wouldn't miss it. She was worried that he might. What would being a teenager be like in the age of Covid. Either way, they were going to find out together.

Sabrina hoped Elsbeth wouldn't remember last year's Covid strained birthday party; there was no way Sabrina was going to host a tea party birthday with six giggling guests even if they all promised to wear face masks. How could the world expect them to? "You okay?" she asked Elsbeth. "Got everything you need?" Elsbeth nodded; she was preoccupied with squirting water from one yellow ducky onto another yellow ducky. Sabrina got to her feet; she left the bathroom door slightly ajar as she headed back to the kitchen.

She could hear Harold laughing heartily. She could hardly distinguish one hand-held transceiver from another, but she would bet he was using the newly purchased hand-held. It would take Harold a good forty-five minutes to call everyone on the net, and after that some of the hams would hang around for a rag-chew. Harold was so at ease with his time on the ham net. It was clear relaxation for him. Sort of like knitting for her.

Back at the table in front of her laptop Sabrina was unable to concentrate – was lack of ability to concentrate one of the early signs of Covid? Brain fog? There were too many things that needed her attention – which to work on first?

She finally decided to make a list: - Nathan's birthday, a significant watershed which would put a teen-ager in the house; - Elsbeth's birthday without a party; - talk to Harold about Nathan; - talk to Harold about new radio equipment they couldn't afford; - write out instructions for tomorrow evening's meal; - determine whether tomorrow was an in-school day for either Nathan or Elsbeth; - thank Nana; - decide whether to order new yarn inventory or notify the landlord that she was closing the shop . . . She was surprised that she could even write out the question. How stark. But, she thought, it belongs here, now. It was an immediate question that she – they – needed to think through. She wanted the yarn shop to thrive, survive. But not at the cost of the family. She decided that tomorrow, with mask on and disinfecting wipes in hand, she would run into the pharmacy to purchase more vitamin D tablets.

Putting her new list aside, she clicked on to the yarn shop website. Managing the website was at the farside of her computer capability, but it was critical to keeping the scant flow of online orders. Like seeds started for a new spring garden, it needed care. And then her mind was wandering off again – wouldn't it be more economical to order in bulk from Logan Paper Goods some boxes and big padded envelopes for shipping orders than depending on what the post office had on hand? Making an executive decision without the need to put it in her to-do list, she quickly found the Logan Paper Goods website and placed a curbside order. Logan's used to be downtown, but they had re-located totally to their overtown warehouse.

Seeming to be in a hurry, Harold laid his hand-held down on the table.

"Rag-chew over?"

"No. Ran out of battery. I was able to 73. I can recharge it overnight." Harold was already back in the hallway. "Elsbeth's getting out of the tub. She wants me to tuck her in." The last of Harold's sentence was lost in Elsbeth's giggles.

Sabrina picked up the hand-held, hardly bigger than an individual serving cereal box. She had seen Harold snap the battery lid off a hand-held with his thumbnail, something she was never able to do. She pried the battery lid open with the prong of a banker's clip; she wrote the battery type along the side of her notebook page. She was planning a sweet surprise for her husband. Today had been a better day at the yarn shop than expected. She needed to let him know "Thank you" too; what he did let her do the things she did. They were good partners. Elsbeth's excited chatter filled the house, but Harold was answering with a slow, calming moderate voice. Nathan, maintaining silence, closed his laptop and left the table. Sabrina switched from the website to Facebook.

Sabrina thought she knew all the followers on her Facebook account, even though some of them used inventive nicknames. She laughed at a post from Abbey Reynolds. "Finally finished my first mukluk with double points. Starting on the second. I'll have a perfect set if I can remember all the mistakes I made on the first."

Another poster was quick to respond. "Oh, how I miss being able to sit around and help each other. You wouldn't have made so many mistakes if you'd been at Sabrina's Circle."

Sabrina liked the reference to a knitting circle. She posted a comment of her own. "Don't despair, ladies, AND gentlemen, Sabrina's Circle will be back. Covid be . . . well, you know." She noted she had a new follower, Lolly, whom she couldn't place.

Harold came back into the room so quietly she did not realize at first that he was looking over her shoulder. "You've got a loyal crew of followers – you must be doing something right." He gave Sabrina a quick rub on her shoulder. Putting on his jacket, he left the house by the backdoor; he would be making his nightly round of the house and inspection up and down the street. She shut down her laptop and went to put on her night clothes. On her way, she peeked into Nathan's room.

When Harold came back inside she whispered, "Nathan is sound asleep, but still in his clothes. We better wake him up so he can get his pajamas on."

"Leave him be," Harold whispered.

In the dark of their bedroom Sabrina asked the question she had long held off. "What are we going to do about Nathan's escapade today?" Harold did not immediately answer, but Sabrina could tell that he had not fallen asleep.

"Do you ever remember me saying anything about Candace Phipps? I went to school with her. She's some kind of psychiatrist at the hospital."

"I don't remember her."

"The other day when I was installing their new vending machines she came by. She said they were seeing all kinds of strange mental issues with the children Covid patients. Like the kids were having trouble understanding what was going on around them. Things they couldn't process." He paused. "I don't know. Maybe their parents are uneasy about what's going on so much that they can't seem to help their children. I think we – you and me – have tried to stay balanced, but I'm sure the kids . . . Look at what Elsbeth talked about tonight, and Nathan probably knows we've been worried. Hell, we are worried. Everything is new to Elsbeth, but Nathan remembers last year, even before that." Harold sighed as he finished. "Nathan's almost a teen-ager," Harold said, seemingly surprised.

"So, you don't think we should do anything by way of punishment?"

"No, but I don't know exactly what direction we should be going. Is tomorrow an in-school day for him?"

"Yes. I checked the school calendar. I'll take him in the morning. I'll take Elsbeth with me tomorrow, too. Give Nana a break."

"You can imagine the toll this is taking on the school administrators, especially the teachers." Harold plumped his pillow under his neck.

Sometime in the night Nathan woke up. When he appeared in the kitchen in the morning he was in his pajamas. When Sabrina told him that she would be dropping him off at school he only nodded. Harold left a little earlier than normal. On his way through the kitchen he patted Nathan on the shoulder, said "Nate" softly, and kissed Elsbeth on the top of the head. "See you at supper," he called as he went out the door.

As Sabrina dropped Nathan at school she was reassured by the line of cars and the appearance of other children arriving. She tried to think of something positive to say as good-bye, but that wasn't an automatic reminder of the day before. She came up with: "Make it a great day, Nathan." She could see his little smile over his shoulder as he hurried away from the parent car.

Logan's Paper Goods did not appear to be open, but when she stopped in front and called the number on her mobile phone, a male voice said her order was ready and he would bring it out immediately. She recognized Mr. Logan himself. "I couldn't tell if you were open," Sabrina said. "This is the first time I've been here since you left downtown. You need to have some outside signs . . . or something. Maybe OPEN TO THE PUBLIC, and a new special every day. You look too much like a warehouse."

"Maybe you're right," Mr. Logan said. "Thank you for your business. How are yarn sales going?"

"Not nearly as good as I would hope."

"Well, when I slow down long enough to knit, I know where to go to get my gear." Spoken like a true fisherman thought Sabrina, and then smiling to herself, you never know, Mr. Logan, we may hook you into knitting yet!

A few blocks from Logan's Sabrina realized she was close to what the radio hams called the candy store. They had everything and then some that a radio ham could dream of. Even some radio toys – or 'candy' they didn't know they needed, yet. Rolling her car to a stop, she noticed a sign for curbside delivery. Using her mobile phone again, she looked at her notebook and asked the candy store clerk about availability of an

Ni-MH.

"We have them by the dozens. What radio do you want it for?"

"For my husband's handi-talky."

"Did he buy it here? We probably have the record. What's his call sign?"

"KDØRVQO."

"Yeah, Harold Harkins. Give me a sec . . . He probably wants it for his FT60. It's here on the shelf somewhere. Is this cash or credit card?"

"Credit card."

A stout man with scant grey hair protruding from beneath his tractor hat emerged from the candy store. So this was the candyman. He was balancing several items in his hands; he passed the small battery box through the door to Sabrina and began punching on the screen of a small tablet. Sabrina gave him her credit card. She noticed his lapel pin call sign, "KØCBTO? I think I've heard you on the net that Harold calls."

"That would be me. Has Harold talked you into getting your own license one of these days?"

"He's sort of given up."

"Yeah. My wife finally gave in and studied for her ticket. She's not as active as I am, but sometimes she hits a streak. Here, I need you to sign here." He steadied the tablet on the lower edge of the open window.

Signing on the tiny screen, Sabrina wondered if anyone would really be able to read her name.

"Thank you," KØCBTO said. He began patting his hand on the jacket of his upper chest clothing, eventually pulling out a wrapped lollipop which he offered to Elsbeth. "They don't call this the candy store for nothing."

The clerk was back in the store before Sabrina examined the figures on the little slip of paper he had given her. Forty-five dollars! She had not calculated that a new battery would be so expensive; how close was she getting to her credit card limit? The new normal was taking its toll.

Sabrina turned on the lights when she and Elsbeth entered the shop, but she locked the door behind her. She was well ahead of her scheduled opening time, so she was surprised at the knock on the front door. Sally Voyles, whom she had not seen in a long time, was tapping on the glass.

"I saw the lights on," the middle-aged woman said from behind a purple mask, "so I knew someone was inside. I need some more red yarn. The Pandemic didn't stop everything. People still keep getting cancer." Sally toed the threshold, but remained outside.

Sabrina quickly collected three skeins of red, printed out an invoice and was soon back at the door. Using her handbag as a steady surface, Sally wrote out a check. "Thank you so much," Sally said. "Saved me an extra trip. I was going to come by later for a curbside pickup, but," she stepped back, "I guess we could call this a sidewalk sale."

"That's about right," Sabrina smiled. And remembered to say, "Thank you for your business," as she watched Sally cross the street.

Sabrina was so deep in thought about what she needed to do to save her business that she almost missed the neon flashing light bulbs going off right in front of her. If it is possible for a person's thoughts to do a double take, Sabrina's brain jolted. There might as well have been cartoon arrows in the sky pointing at her head. Yes! That is about right! Muse in the form of a customer. She'll have to thank Sally sometime for the moment of clarity. Yes, a good old-fashioned tried-and-true don't-need-to-re-invent-anything sidewalk sale! What an idea! All outdoors. Easy enough to practice social distancing. No tricks, no gimmicks, just good old fashioned customer service with a Covid-beating plan. A sidewalk sale. But when?

"Elsbeth, come with me." In a flash they were back out of the store and on their way to city hall. Sabrina had been there before, was somewhat acquainted with the clerk who issued business permits. And especially sidewalk sale permits.

The clerk was a bit hesitant. She wasn't always sure what the latest health mandate required.

"I don't know how the city, or the county, or the state decided what were so-called essential businesses, but they haven't said a thing about sidewalk sales," Sabrina declared.

"Well, no."

"Then I want a permit for a three-day sidewalk sale." If no one else is going to start something, thought Sabrina, I will. I have a business to run. And a family to feed. And a dream to catch while I am at it. She was off and running. She didn't know how fast she was running, but she was beginning to hear the countdown clock ticking.

DAYL

Chapter Six

Dayl Carruthers had nothing to do all day but watch the street. If the weather was tolerable, he sat in a rocker on his porch.

If the weather was less agreeable, he sat inside behind the white gauze curtains that his late wife, Eloise Mae, Emmie, had sewn for their tidy, little house she kept so well. "Let's you see outside perfectly good, but no one can see in," Emmie had said the day she put them up.

The street had a regular schedule – almost – that Dayl was accustomed to. Of course things were different now that the Pandemic had set in, but still there was a lot of movement that was normal and repetitive. Some workers left their houses in the early morning hours, often with children to be taken to school, and returned in the late afternoon. In between were the FedEx and UPS and other delivery trucks or vans. There were more deliveries at some houses than at others, but Dayl was quite aware of an upsurge in home deliveries since the Covid set in. He had taken up waving at the drivers.

He was also certain in his own mind that he had at least once thwarted the plans of a porch pirate. The FedEx driver had delivered three huge boxes at a house two doors down only moments before a sedan Dayl had never seen before stopped at the curb. No one got out of the car for several minutes. When a woman finally got out of the passenger side and looked cautiously up and down the street Dayl picked up a pair of garden gloves from the hallway table and casually stepped outside. He let the door close loudly. Without looking in the stranger's direction, he examined the grass at the edge of the driveway. He thought maybe he heard a voice call from within the car; the woman stopped mid-stride and returned to the car which quickly sped away. As the car passed Dayl's driveway, he noted the license plate. H4C TK53. He never saw the car in the neighborhood again.

This morning, the weather was bearable. Dayl was sitting outside in his rocker, but he was definitely uncomfortable. His granddaughter, Tressa, whose college had closed all in-person classes, wanted to continue her remote learning at his house. She didn't feel she could go home because her parents were in quarantine, and a younger sibling was probably already ill with the danged virus. He had reluctantly decided he would call her later in the morning and give her permission to come.

He didn't understand why he was reluctant to have her at the house. Tressa had been a frequent guest, but that was when Emmie was still alive and there were so many things they could do together. He had no idea what he would do to entertain his granddaughter. Dayl had never been a good entertainment committee.

His neighbor, Anna, didn't understand his anxieties. She had been quite pleased at the news. "Oh, it will be good to see her again."

"What can I do about meals?" Dayl had worried.

"I'll bet she knows how to cook. You might even gain back some of that weight you've been losing."

"But what can I do to entertain her?"

"She won't need any entertainment if she is on remote learning. My grandson, Nathan, is only in the seventh grade, but his remote learning lessons keep him busy most of the day. I worry about it, he should be getting more exercise instead of being glued to a chair all day," he remembered Anna saying.

Thinking about Nathan, he couldn't remember seeing a Harkins car yet this morning, making it likely that Nathan was actually in school, and Anna was alone. He sprung up from his chair with the sudden urge to invite himself for coffee. Anna had helped him in more ways than he could count when Emmie was ill, and then when Emmie was gone, Anna had helped him fend off the loneliness when his family was not available. Anna had been a great friend of Emmie's, now she was a great friend to him.

He didn't want to be married again, and hoped she didn't consider the time they spent together a prelude to a proposal. Nonetheless, he rattled around alone in a house far too big for one person. And full of memories. Maybe if he moved, he wouldn't be haunted by constant images of Emmie. He had faithfully visited a former golf buddy at a nursing home. With one breath the buddy had urged Dayl to make the move to join him and with the next breath had complained about the poor quality of the food, or the lack of attention, or too much attention at the wrong time. And now that the Pandemic had invaded all their lives a person would be a fool to move in with a bunch of high-risk individuals. He poked around the kitchen cabinets for a bit, but before he started looking he knew that he would find no cookies or crackers suitable to take with him over to Anna's. He picked up his mask but left it dangling around his ear.

Empty coffee mug in hand, he presented himself at Anna's side door and knocked gently, as neighbors do. Her mobile phone hanging from her wrist, Anna opened the door; Dayl had the distinct impression that Anna was preparing to leave the house. "Looks like you're going somewhere." He started to back away.

"I was. But I'd rather see you." She walked over to check something on the stove, sat her purse in a chair and took off her heavy sweater. "So, what's going on in your world?"

"I'm going to call Tressa this morning and tell her she can

come."

"Good. You won't regret it. She'll be good company." Anna was banging things around on the kitchen counter. "Drat! My teakettle isn't working. We'll have to have microwave coffee this morning."

Dayl had started to seat himself, but he rose again and moved to the counter. "What's the problem?"

"I don't know. Doesn't seem to want to heat this morning." Anna had her head in the refrigerator.

Dayl began experimentally moving the teakettle and wiggling the plug. "Here's your problem – it wasn't making good contact with the outlet."

"Oh, thank you. I thought it was a goner. I was going to look online for a new electric teakettle. I really like how they shut themselves off." She poked something into the oven and came to stand next to Dayl at the counter. "I should have looked at the connection before going into panic mode." Anna disappeared into the dining room.

Dayl sat down at the far side of the kitchen table with his back to the window. He knew he could trust Anna to serve him a good cup of coffee, honest coffee, with none of those ramboisterous, ersatz, jollied-up flavors. People who insisted on added additions to their addictive drinks weren't the coffee lovers they claimed to be. He had watched Anna take a jar of powdered coffee from an upper cabinet and thought to himself to try to remember to put powdered coffee on his grocery list so he wouldn't always be coming to Anna's house empty-handed. He thought cookies too; and whatever it was that a college girl needed. He could hear sounds of a printer running.

Anna came back with several pieces of paper in her hand. "I don't think Nathan would mind if I showed these to you." She laid one of the sheets of paper on the table in front of Dayl. "I thought some of these were rather clever. It's part of his homework for his art class – design a mask." She studied a second sheet briefly before laying it down for Dayl to see.

"Hmmmmm." Dayl turned the first art example upside down.

"Wonder if Nathan would design a mask for me?"

"What would yours look like?"

Dayl answered quickly. "I would have a cowboy on his horse looking off into a big valley. Maybe it would be Gene Autrey, or Roy Rogers."

"Or maybe you," Anna said watching closely to see if he smiled, and then added: "I think the school is providing blank masks for the students. They're having a creative art competition. Teachers have had to be pretty inventive." Anna shuffled through the sheets. "He made one for me . . . here it is . . . pink and purple tulips. Actually, I've ordered one online. The Mona Lisa wearing a mask. No more speculation about her enigmatic smile." Anna laid the remainder of the sheets on the table, motioned for Dayl to push his coffee mug toward her and filled it three-quarters full. Anna knew that Dayl could drink his coffee without any sweetener, but he loved to finish filling the mug with cream."

Dayl laughed. "Maybe I'll order one for myself. A singing cowboy."

"Are you doing the singing?"

"Why not? I was in my college choir." Dayl was beginning to smell something quite delicious. When Anna set a small plate with two cinnamon rolls hot from the oven down in front of him, he pretended to swoon. "I must have been a very good boy to deserve this."

"Have you ever thought about selling your house and moving?" Nana asked abruptly.

Dayl didn't answer right away. "No . . . have you?"

"I've thought about it. I'm sure my children would be happy to see me in a care facility."

"We can see what a bad idea that has turned out to be."

"There's so much maintenance, I could afford a little bit of help, but where can you find reliable people?" She took a bite of her cinnamon roll. "Harold and Sabrina don't know, don't tell them, but I've been talking to a real estate salesperson. He's apparently found a couple of properties he wants me to look at."

"In Overlake?" Dayl felt alarmed at the thought that Anna could move.

"Close to Overlake. Actually, I was looking before the Pandemic." Anna stopped at a knock on the side door. Dayl could not see who was outside when Anna opened the door, but he immediately recognized the voice.

"Hi, Mrs. Harkins, remember me? I'm Tressa. Do you know where my grandfather is? His house is unlocked –"

Anna opened the door more widely. "Of course I remember you. It hasn't been that long since the last time I saw you. Your grandfather is right here."

Tressa started to sweep around the chairs to reach for her grandfather but stopped abruptly and hugged herself. She looked apologetically at Anna. "I'll try to remember to stay six feet away." She looked at her grandfather again. "This hug is for you. One for both of you."

Dayl mimicked his granddaughter, and thought to himself how beautiful she was, her short hair dark and curly. She must have gotten all her good genes from her mother's side of the family. Dayl was afraid that his son, Tressa's father, had inherited his hair genes and would soon be partially bald.

"I'm sorry I hadn't gotten around to calling you about coming," said Dayl. "I was just telling Anna, Mrs. Harkins, the news...."

"And I'm sorry that I didn't give you the chance. I hope it is alright. But they were throwing everyone out of the dorms. It was here or home," said Tressa.

Anna placed another small plate with a cinnamon roll at the end of the table. "You're in luck. Your grandfather didn't eat all of the goodies. You will need to help him polish up his sociability."

"Oh, yum." Tressa glanced again at her grandfather. "Thank you for letting me come. Mom and Dad both say they're getting better, but Trent and Boyd are both showing early symptoms. They were all so careful, Mom made the boys move to the basement, but looks like they both caught it anyway."

"That's too bad," Anna offered. She placed a full coffee mug in front of Tressa. "Cream? Sugar? Stevia?" Anna set a small plastic container with a green pop-up lid in front of Tressa.

Tressa used the tip of her spoon for handling a few grains of stevia. "Too much makes it taste awful. That's why some people don't like it."

"So, your college is going online? That will really be hard for some classes."

"I think it will take the faculty a little time to get it all organized." She looked at her grandfather. "It was just crazy. Look out the window at my car. There was hardly room for me to drive. They told us to take everything we could carry and not to come back. My roommate didn't have a car, so she loaded me down, and then another . . . friend . . . crammed in a lot of his stuff . . . I hope I can unload some of it temporarily in your garage. Until they can come get it."

Dayl thought his granddaughter had almost said boyfriend, but he wouldn't ask her about that yet. "I've got some stuff I need to get rid of, but we can make room."

Anna poured more coffee into Dayl's mug. "I forget what you're majoring in, Tressa," she said.

"I'm not totally committed, but I think I'm pre-med."

"Your grandfather is not a very good cook," Dayl suddenly said.

"Not to worry. I can open a can with the best of them."

"I don't have a can opener that works anymore," Dayl lied.

"You are in bad shape," Anna lamented. She got up and rummaged around in one of the under-counter drawers. "Here. I have a GI can opener I can loan you."

"I haven't seen one of these in a long time." Dayl twisted the two little pieces of hinged metal. "Maybe you'll come have lunch with us some day."

"It'll have to be one of the days I don't have Nathan or Elsbeth."

"They're welcome, too." Dayl rose from his chair and put his small plate into the sink. "You don't have them today and you were on the way out of the house when I came over." He looked at his granddaughter. "We better be on our way and let Anna get started on her errands."

Tressa followed her grandfather's example and left her mug and plate in the sink. "Delicious cinnamon rolls. I'll have to get your recipe."

Anna lifted a can of cinnamon spice and a shaker of nutmeg. "Any frozen rolls packet from the grocer's, plus your own special, secret ingredients." Anna spoke like a co-conspirator. And smiled.

On their way back to the Carruthers house, they walked past Tressa's Volkswagen.

"Good grief, girl, there's hardly room for a driver. You've driven all night. We can get you unpacked after you've had a nap. There's still a bed in your father's old room." Dayl hesitated. "With no one to fuss at me, things have gotten pretty messy."

Dayl intended to start moving things around in the garage while Tressa napped, but he fell asleep in his chair by the front door waiting for the mail carrier. When he woke up there was a newspaper poking up out of the box and he realized the letter carrier – male or female – had come and gone without a sound. The newspaper was a weekly from the town where Emmie was born; Dayl never expected to recognize any names, but he enjoyed reading the editorials written by the crusty old editor. He had hardly gotten started on cleaning a section of the garage when Tressa appeared, amazingly bright-eyed for such a short nap. Dayl motioned along a part of the wall. "I thought I'd clear out this junk to make room for your junk."

"Well, here, I can help you. Where are you putting your junk?"

"Against the back, there under the window. I'm culling out as I go."

Tressa started energetically moving boxes and other items. Curious about one thing she found leaning against the wall, she asked. "Where's the rest of it?" She held up a single wheel with attached pedals.

Dayl smiled at her bafflement. "Haven't you ever seen one of these before? It's a unicycle. I used to be pretty good at it." He snugged the wheel against his armpit and turned the pedals with one hand.

"With just one wheel?"

"Yep. That's why it's called a unicycle. Used to always see them at circuses. My lodge had a whole unit of unicyclists. We were quite a sensation."

"You rode this?"

"Darn tootin' I did. Drove your grandmother crazy. I'd like to show you but I'd probably crack my skull. Or something."

"Could I learn how to do it?"

"I don't even want you to try. Your mother would never forgive me if you fell, got a concussion." He gave the wheel another turn. He was beginning to feel uneasy about the gleam in Tressa's eyes. "Or broke your something." Somehow, he had to get the unicycle removed from his premises. He pulled his mobile phone from his pocket and checked if he had on his contact list the number of his lodge buddy, Vince, who was running facilities at Overlake Hospital. "My old lodge partner was asking me not long ago if I still had my unicycle. He must have had a reason for wanting to know. Maybe they are trying to rebuild the unit." When Vince answered Dayl pushed the speaker button.

Vince seemed preoccupied and puzzled by the call. "Your unicycle?"

"Vince, you were asking if I could find my old unicycle."

"When did I do that?"

Dayl looked at his watch and walked out of the garage into the driveway. "I can bring it to you early this afternoon." He clicked the speaker function off.

"Look, Dayl, I don't remember any conversation about unicycles and I'm pretty busy right now. Could we talk again this evening?"

"I'll be there in twenty minutes. Where will I find you?"

"I'm in the covered parking garage, but I'd rather postpone

this until later."

"I'll be there right away. My car, my granddaughter driving," Dayl announced and clicked the END icon. "Come on, Tressa, we'll take Vince's unicycle to him and get a fast-food meal on our way back. You know the way to the hospital? He says he's in the covered parking garage."

Tressa knew the way to the hospital, but the scene that met Dayl's eyes was far from what he expected. The open areas around the garage were full of cars, but the covered parking section was cordoned off with yellow tape and orange warning cones. There were several men with tape measures moving around under the roof. Hardly recognizable with hard hat and mask, Vince ducked under the tape and came to the passenger side of the car.

Dayl pulled his mask up to cover his nose and exclaimed, "Holy cow! What's going on?" He stepped out from the passenger seat, opened the back door and handed the unicycle to Vince. "Sorry. I had forgotten I still had it."

Vince somewhat reluctantly accepted the unicycle and immediately handed it off to a young man who had followed him.

"How've you been, Vince? I sure miss our regular lodge meetings."

"I've been spending so much time here at the hospital I haven't been able to connect with anybody on Zoom." To Dayl, Zoom was just another one of those computer things that was moving way faster than he wanted to.

Dayl waved his arm at all the activity under the roof. "What's going on?"

"We're converting the garage into a temporary hospital. Covid is over-running us."

"I hadn't heard the hospital was at capacity . . ." Dayl's attention was distracted by the fair-haired young man who had started away with the unicycle. The young man appeared to be comparing the height of the unicycle seat to his leg.

"We've been over capacity a couple of days, turned some patients away. The retired CEO turned up yesterday with his plans for a temporary expansion into the garage." He looked past Dayl at Tressa. "You've got a chauffeur?"

"Yes. My granddaughter, Tressa." Dayl couldn't take his eyes off the young man who was rolling the unicycle into the garage.

"Didn't you have a granddaughter going into medicine?"

"Yes, that's her."

Tressa leaned forward to nod at Vince. She reached out as if to shake his hand, and thought better of it, prepared to fist bump.

"How's it going? Medical school?"

"I'm not there yet. Actually, my classes have closed down, so I've come to Grandpa's for a few days while the online classes get worked out."

"You could come to work at the hospital," Vince suggested. "We're short of staff everywhere. Give you a taste of real medicine."

"I'm supposed to be in a 14-day quarantine."

"You've been exposed?"

"Not that I know of."

"We need you here. As long as your temperature's normal." Vince turned to walk away. "Think about it. Start tomorrow morning. See Judy Kaviski in HR at 9 am sharp."

Vince was interrupted by a gasp from Dayl. The young man had attempted to mount the unicycle and instantly found himself launched at the pavement. "You're going to have to take that unicycle away from that guy."

Shrugging, Vince was nonchalant. "That's my son. He's home because his classes are suspended, too. He just needs some coaching. He's ridden my unicycle before." Vince was gone with a wave.

TRESSA

Chapter Seven

Tressa was surprised and pleased that her grandfather was willing to concede the driving to her.

When he asked if she knew where the Overlake Hospital was, she said she did – she thought she did – for fear he would change his mind. She was relieved when the upper floors of the hospital came into view. Even at a distance it was obvious that something was happening at the covered parking garage.

She was aware of the man in navy blue work clothing with a hospital logo who stepped under the yellow warning tape to come to meet the car, but she had more interest in the young man in jeans and a blue flannel jacket who was several steps behind. The mask he wore had a colorful logo she couldn't read.

Tressa watched as Dayl removed the unicycle from the back seat, and was amused at the alacrity with which Vince handed the singular wheel to the younger man. He had that comfortably responsible air about him.

The young man assessed the unicycle as he rolled it into the garage. She was not surprised when he tried to mount the seat and admired the way he nimbly jumped to the pavement when he was not able to gain a balance. She looked back at her grandfather again when she realized she had become the topic of their conversation. She didn't want to explain that she was still undecided about becoming a doctor, so she simply said, "I'm not there yet."

She was surprised at Vince Garretson's mention of working at the hospital. They had been told when they fled from the college that they should expect to be in a 14-day quarantine. She knew, however, that hospital staffs all across the country were critically short-handed. Health providers themselves had become ill with the virus and those who weren't sick were worn down with fatigue and long hours.

The young man with the unicycle was still in Tressa's line of vision and she could see, even before her grandfather's gasp, that his second attempt to ride the single wheel had turned to a disaster. "Is he hurt?" she asked, her voice showing more alarm than she wanted to.

Vince, who had only witnessed the aftermath of the precipitous fall, turned back toward the car. "He better not be. If he's broken something, he's fired. He's my son, Jay," he said to Dayl, and then to Tressa he finished with, "His college is closed for the time being, too."

Tressa tried to keep a concerned look on her face, but it was hard not to smile. Without asking, she had learned both his name and his relationship to Vince. As she put the car in motion to leave, she could see that Jay had gotten on his feet, was removing his flannel jacket and was examining his elbow.

"Let's get some food to take home," Dayl suggested. "What would you like?"

"JimPops? They make really good hamburgers." She didn't mention the pineapple and strawberry milk shakes.

With two hamburgers, a super order of waffle fries, and Tressa's favorite milk shake they sat down for a late meal in the kitchen that would forever remind Tressa of her grandmother, Emmie.

"After we get your car unloaded, I want you to help me clear the daybed and part of the closet in . . . your grandmother's sewing room. She loved quilting. She was always pleased when she was helping you with a quilting project. You'll be more comfortable in the sewing room."

"I remember," Tressa choked. Neither one of them was able to speak for a few moments. Tressa swallowed down several gulps of the shake. "I'll be happy to help with the bed later in the afternoon, after I get back from the hospital."

"The hospital?" Dayl was baffled. Vince had said something about tomorrow.

"I'm going to put in an application right now. Could I use your name as a reference?"

Dayl was still processing her first statement. "Of course."

"And Mrs. Harkins, next door? Do you think she would mind if I gave them her name?"

"I'm sure it would be okay with Anna. I can mention it to her." Dayl was pretty sure Tressa was in if she wanted to be. His friend Vince was a doer not a talker. Dayl was very happy to learn that Tressa had grown up to lean forward and was not leaving everything to chance. A lot like what he always loved about Emmie.

Having finished her hamburger, Tressa rose from the table. "I'll need to change into something more presentable." She brought a suitcase from her car and carried it into the sewing room. She had noticed that her grandfather had made some changes in the house after her grandmother's death, but the sewing room had not been touched. Had she known she would be applying for a job she would have chosen other things from her closet to bring with her. As it was, she dressed in the only dark slacks she had brought with her, a white cotton blouse and a soft blue sweater-jacket.

She would need to enter the hospital from the front, but she drove past the parking garage first. She was disappointed not to see Jay. She thought she saw his father with some workmen deep in the garage. The only parking space she could find was on the street over a block from the entrance. She locked the car, walked a few steps away, abruptly turned on her heel and went back to her car; she had forgotten her mask, a bright cherry red that did nothing to compliment her clothing.

There were paper notices posted all over the front doors, most of them prohibiting visitors. Tressa pushed her way through the heavy glass doors. The lobby was completely empty, no one at the reception desk near the front doors. Tressa looked around for some signage, something that would give her a clue about where she should go.

A woman with a clear plastic face shield that hung from a helmet-like device on her head hurried from one corridor to another. Belatedly, she noted Tressa's presence. "Oh, I'm sorry, we're not open to visitors." She pointed toward the signs on the doors.

"I'm not a visitor," Tressa said. "I've come to apply for a job."

The woman looked blank for a few seconds. "A job? Oh, a job. Lord knows we can use all the help we can get. Human Resources. Human Resources. They're down this hall. Ask for Judy." She pointed to the corridor she had just left. She turned around and offered, "Here, come with me."

On the other side of a window-wall were several desks, only one of them occupied by a woman wearing a headset in front of a computer. She nodded a greeting to Tressa and pushed a sheet of paper through the opening at the bottom of a glass panel. Tressa studied the paper form, which appeared to refer primarily to nursing staff. She pushed the paper back and waited for the woman to speak to her. The woman's mask had slid down her face and hung around her neck; there were dark arcs under her eyes. Slowly, the woman pulled one of the earpieces away from the side of her head and looked at Tressa.

"I'm not a nurse. I'm hoping to be a doctor, but I am applying for a job. I've been a hospital aide before."

"You're not a nurse? Sorry. That's what we need the worst."

A white-coated doctor came into the room from a side door and turned a confused look at the Human Resources clerk. "Is Judy here? Judy Kaviski? Gone on a break?"

"Gone home. Tested positive. Judy says she doesn't feel bad and is trying to work from home. Whatcha got? I can get it to her."

"Thanks." The doctor laid some papers on the clerk's desk and was gone in a nano-second.

The clerk looked again at Tressa. "Had any experience in a hospital?"

"I was a volunteer aide two summers when I was in high school. And I am pre-med." In for a penny, in for a pound she thought. "My college sent all of us home for distance learning."

"Think you could be a floor aide?"

"Yes, I do." Not exactly the career path she envisioned, but a movement in the right direction.

"You're hired." The clerk pulled open a desk drawer and selected several forms. "How soon could you start?"

"Anytime. Now."

The clerk pushed the papers under the glass panel and turned her attention back to her computer screen.

A tall, middle-aged woman in a uniform with an RN name tag zoomed into the room and came to stand near Tressa. "Is this one of the new nurses we are expecting?"

"No. And I don't think we're going to see them, either."

The RN lowered her voice. "Is this applicant a nurse?" Without waiting for an answer she turned to Tressa, "Are you a nurse?"

"No." The work was vital; you were put to work. Work first, paperwork to follow. No ceremony to stand on. It reminded Tressa, too, of how her brother, Trent, would brag of his athletic adventures. She smiled and could hear him say "next man up" when he would tell the story of subbing into the game for an injured teammate. Someone needed to step up to get the job done. And he would smile so big when he would say he made the game winning shot. She was doing him one better: next woman up. She would have to tell him.

"No. I haven't read her application yet, she's still filling it out," Human Resources told the RN, "but I think she will qualify as a floor aide. I'm going to give her an auxiliary jacket."

They were talking about Tressa as if she weren't there. "What floor are you putting her on?"

"How about the fourth floor? Can you use her there?"

"How soon can you get her papers done?"

"You're almost done, aren't you?" The Human Resources clerk asked Tressa, and at Tressa's nod she directed her instructions to the RN. "Take her down to the auxiliary room to help her pick out a jacket and when you get back she'll be good to go."

Things were moving almost too fast for Tressa, but she followed the RN farther down the corridor.

"My name's Tilley. Grace Tilley," the RN said. "All the auxiliary activities are suspended," Nurse Tilley said.

"I'm Tressa Carruthers."

"You live here in town?"

"My grandfather does."

Tressa felt Nurse Tilley's eyes examining her. "You must be Eloise Mae's granddaughter.

"Emmie? Yes, I am."

Nurse Tilley looked carefully at Tressa again. "She was a lovely person. We could all see how hard her passing was on your grandfather." The nurse didn't bother to connect the dots. She opened the door to a large, cluttered room. "The hospital suspended the auxiliary activities almost at the beginning – too risky – too hard to keep testing all the coming and going. Some of the auxiliary members were quite angry. We were able to hire some of them to staff, the president was one. She works in day surgery for us. She's here twice the hours she gets paid for." Nurse Tilley led Tressa to a clothing rack, hung with identical light green jackets. "Pick out a couple that fit you." Her mobile phone in hand, Nurse Tilley walked out into the corridor. Tressa could still hear her talking but tried not to listen to the details.

The green jackets were all freshly washed and pressed, and hanging by random order both by size and name embroidered on the left front. Tressa found two jackets that felt like a good fit. She still was wearing one of the jackets when Nurse Tilley came back into the room.

"Oh, you've picked out Mary Teffelt's jackets. I thought you were about her size."

"Won't she be upset at someone else wearing her jackets?"

"Mary's passed away. She left this world a little after your grandmother died. Mary was a wonder, though, one of our best auxiliary members. We're using the jackets during this Pandemic pinch. That way the regular staff will be able to identify you and not ask you to do anything beyond your . . . credentials." While they were talking Nurse Tilley had led Tressa back to Human Resources. "Do you have a name tag for Tressa? Something so people won't be calling her Mary Teffelt."

The Human Resources clerk giggled. "You remember what Mary Teffelt's friends called her? Mary Teflon. I need to get Tressa's signatures. I'll make her a name tag and send her up. "Shouldn't be too long."

"Good. I'll find someone she can shadow until she gets acquainted with our procedures."

The world was moving at a faster clip than Tressa expected. When she had replied to the Human Resources clerk's question of when she would be available to work she wished she had been more specific. Apparently when she said she was available any time the clerk had interpreted it to mean this afternoon. Well, she could use the money. Her parents had been making sacrifices to get her through college without her acquiring student loan debt. The Human Resources clerk nodded when Tressa returned the signed documents. The clerk pulled the head phones off one ear to tell Tressa that the elevator to the fourth floor was in the main lobby. Tressa had joined the medical ranks in the war against Covid. It was all a little bit like her grandfather's description of his wartime service. If something needed to be done, and you could do it, you just might get ordered in to fill the line. Being drafted was beginning to take on meaning to her.

Tressa passed the hospital gift shop, now closed and eerily darkened. She found the elevator easily enough, but she had a sense of disorientation because everything was on a diagonal. Along one hallway a giant arrow pointed to the parking garage;

someone had tried to cover it with long pieces of tape. Ignoring the warning, Tressa followed the direction of the arrow.

The building exit that led to the garage was covered with more tape, but Tressa could see through the glass doors. Vince Garretson stood in front of a group of workers. Next to Vince was a man in a business suit. He was holding open a large sheet of blueprints, with a large roll of blueprints next to him on the garage floor. She was hoping to spot Jay but Jay was not in the garage.

She noted to herself with a smile, a young man adventurous enough to think he could master riding a unicycle was worth getting acquainted with.

Tressa knew she could pick him out of any crowd – he'd be the one covered with bruises.

SABRINA

Chapter Eight

Nathan flew into the kitchen. "Mom! You're burning something," he yelled. From her place at her laptop at the dining room table, Sabrina lifted her head.

What was Nathan shouting about? She could smell nothing burning. Nathan continued creating a commotion. She could hear the oven door slamming shut. She rose from her chair and hastened her step to the kitchen.

Nathan had placed a hot casserole onto the countertop, with nothing under it to protect the counter from the heat. The top of the food – mashed potatoes over the shepherd's pie – was burned black. Nathan was holding his nose. She leaned over, close enough to feel the warmth, but breathed in no offensive smell. Curious. After it cooled off, she could remove the upper layer of blackened mashed potatoes – the rest of it should be perfectly fine. "Are you hungry?" she asked Nathan. She slid a hot pad under the hot casserole dish.

"No. Not now."

"We'll wait for your father." Sabrina went back to her laptop and her stack of notes. With the lockdown she had felt depressed about the future of her yarn shop; the prospect of a socially-distanced sidewalk sale had buoyed her spirits.

Sabrina was putting together her pre-sale inventory list order imagining her wild success. Enough socially distanced customers to catch the interest of the evening news. She would need to make certain that the store was well-stocked with some attractive "special" sidewalk sale items plus all of the backbone stock-in-trade money makers. She was hopeful of moving accessories, too. Needles, some knit-kits, project bags, stitch holders, cable needles, measuring tapes, tiny stitch markers, crochet hooks, gauge converters, swatch rulers, portable swifts. Maybe she could use knitting carry bags as the focus of the sale. And fill them in with some of the slower moving odds and ends. She loved selling lots of natural yarns. She was hoping the sheep and the llamas were going to be able to keep up with the demand. That thought made her smile: all of the animals knowing that they had a role to play in the Covid battle and stepping up to do their part.

She saw she had a text message from Harold. With rising enthusiasm she hit the send button on her order.

Harold's message was a bit annoying: "Don't wait supper, hospital just sent an SOS order to remove vending machines. They're converting the covered parking garage into patient rooms and the machines are in the way of the temporary utility lines."

Sabrina phoned Harold. "They're putting patients in the garage?"

"In the covered lot. They're past max inside. This will be overtime. More dollars in the paycheck. We can use that. I'll just have to make sure they have a new place for the machines. Planners always forget vending machine space. We may not be critical services but we are vital to late hour shift workers."

"I'll leave you a plate in the microwave." She didn't tell him about the burnt food.

Sabrina scraped the burned mashed potato crust off the top of the pie and called the children to supper. She put a generous serving on Elsbeth's plate and pushed the casserole over to Nathan. He spooned a small amount onto his plate and pushed the casserole back to his mother. Tentatively, he forked a small bite and closed his lips over it; after a few chews he made a grimacing swallow. "Mom, this doesn't taste too good."

Reaching into the casserole with her spoon, Sabrina scooped up a healthy portion and put it in her mouth. Tasted all right to her, in fact, didn't seem to have much flavor at all. She tried to remember what seasonings she might have used; with her mind on the yarn order she might have failed to add any seasoning at all. "Tastes okay to me. You want to add a little more salt or pepper?" With the salt shaker she made a quick pass over Elsbeth's plate.

After Nathan finished what little pie he had spooned onto his plate, he brought a loaf of bread and a jar of peanut butter to the table. Abandoning what remained on her plate, Elsbeth finished her meal with a slice of bread and peanut butter too.

The casserole was too big to fit easily in the microwave. Sabrina prepared a plate to be left in the microwave for Harold. There was still plenty of shepherd's pie in the casserole. She covered the casserole with a transparent wrap and found room for it in the refrigerator.

Since their supper had been delayed while they waited for Harold, it was now closer to Elsbeth's bedtime. She hadn't quite gotten Elsbeth in the tub when her mobile phone sounded. She hoped she could ignore it, but when she looked she realized the caller was Yarns Wholesale. "Hello?"

"Hi, Sabrina, this is Sam Ballinger. We've just taken a look at your order..."

"You're still at work? I forget you folks are out on the West Coast."

"Still daylight here ... ah ... this is a pretty big order, bigger than what you have ordered regularly ..."

"Some yarns you don't have in stock?"

"No, we're sitting on some of the biggest inventory we've ever had ... most shops aren't even ordering their normal. Three shops, regular customers of ours, have gone out of business, nailed their doors shut. You seem to be doing fine, maybe we can all learn from you. What's the secret of your success?"

"Well, not yet, but I'm going to have a three-day sidewalk sale in a couple of weeks, and I was getting low on some things."

"A sidewalk sale? You can get a permit for that?"

"The permit clerk said that even with the lockdown no one had told her she couldn't issue a sidewalk permit. It's ideal. Whether people wear masks or not, it's all outdoors. I'll have two long tables on either side of the door and people can easily social distance."

"You know what the weather forecast is that far ahead?"

"Well, no, I don't know that. But I am going to jump out there and just believe it will be excellent. And, if I need 'em, I could probably borrow a couple of those outside heaters from a bar down the street from me. They are barely using them."

"You must be convinced. Or a blind optimist. Either way, I love it," Sam sounded excited. "Do you mind if I share your idea? Our email goes coast to coast."

"Not at all."

"From Yarns Wholesale accept our thanks. And 'Good Luck!' We'll get your order out tomorrow. Send you a confirmation email." The upbeat, positive conversation brought her up. Things were looking good, and helped her feel good for the moment.

Elsbeth had gotten herself out of the tub. With an admonition to Nathan to not stay up too late, Sabrina was in her own bed five minutes after she tucked in Elsbeth. And soon asleep.

But not for long. Before midnight she was awake again. At first she was still drowsy, but alarm set in when she realized Harold was not in bed beside her. Clumsily rising, she toddled to the garage. The vending company van was in its customary location. Padding into the kitchen she checked the microwave; the plate of food she had left for Harold was gone. Absently, she removed a loaf of bread and a jar of peanut butter from the table; she thought she had done that at the end of dinner with the children. But maybe not. Where could Harold be? Cautiously, she opened the door to the basement. Silently creeping halfway down the steps, she could see Harold's hulk on the couch across from the television. But why? The awful thought seized her that perhaps Harold was ill with the feared virus and did not want to expose the rest of the family. She decided not to wake him and padded back to her own bed for the remainder of a fitful night.

Sabrina awakened to the soft sounds of Harold's voice, speaking to her from the doorway. "Hon, I hate to do this, but we're leaving. It's an in-school day for Nathan and I'll drop Elsbeth off at Nana's."

"What?" Sabrina rolled over to face Harold. Her legs ached as she moved.

"I hate to wake you, but I knew you'd be mad if I didn't. How do you feel?"

Sabrina had her legs over the edge of the bed. "I feel fine. Why did you sleep downstairs last night?"

"You looked ... sort of tired. I didn't want to wake you."

Sabrina wasn't sure she wanted to stand up. "Okay. Text me later."

"Will do."

"Tell your mother good-bye." Harold directed his children.

"Oh, wait ... I've got something for you." Sabrina looked futility around the chair on her side of the bed. "Would you bring me my purse? I must have left it in the dining room."

With obvious impatience, Harold found the purse and returned to the bedroom. Sabrina plunged her hand into her purse and withdrew the little cardboard box with the new battery. "I got this for you."

Harold immediately recognized what Sabrina was giving him and sort of collapsed with humble gratitude. He read the printing on the outside of the box. "You got the right one." He was speechless for a few moments. "You knew how to get the right one. You went to the candy store, right?"

"Yes, KØCBTO was very helpful."

"It isn't even my birthday," Harold said by way of protest. He was all but moving in her direction.

"You deserve it. Now get going, Nathan will be late."

The children called from the hallway.

"Good-bye, Mom," from Elsbeth.

"Good-bye, Mom," added Nathan. She thought she heard a little girl voice say "Love you Mom" as the door closed.

Harold followed them for a few steps and then came back to the doorway. He held the battery box in the air. "Thank you isn't near enough."

Sabrina sent him on with a dismissive wave of her hand.

The house was incredibly silent with everyone out for their day. Sabrina slowly dressed, decided to go to the grocery store. They were getting low on milk, and it would be easier to get the shopping done without Elsbeth tagging along. She was dismayed to see Laurin McCurnin drive into the parking lot after her. How could she ever face Laurin again after cowardly sneaking out the grocery cart chute the morning Laurin was engaged in a shouting match with an anti-masker; she decided to slink down behind the wheel and leave as soon as Laurin had entered the store. In vain. Sabrina jumped when she heard a tap on the window, and turned to see Laurin waving at her.

"Are you all right?" Laurin asked. "Are you feeling okay? You haven't fainted?"

A little sheepish about having been discovered by her friend, slowly Sabrina opened the car door and eased out. "How can you ever forgive me for weaseling out the day that old guy was shouting at you?"

Laurin made a gesture of relief. "I'm so glad you did. I didn't want Elsbeth to hear any of it. Did she see him? I really let him have it. It was like a dam or something bursting. I should apologize to you – and everyone – for losing control."

In tandem they moved for the entry doors.

"I don't think Elsbeth saw him," Sabrina said.

"He was just ugly, his bearded face all twisted up. I know she couldn't avoid hearing him." Laurin motioned Sabrina ahead of her.

"I don't think she was listening. The thing that bothered her the most was the fact that we left without groceries, especially ice cream."

"It wasn't really him. It was what he represents. Some of us are that close to losing everything. And they think it is some kind of constitutional experiment." Sabrina could tell Laurin was still in it and could sense her anger rising again. Changing course, Sabrina saw her friend visibly brighten. Laurin laughed. "Where is Elsbeth today?" she asked, and without waiting for an answer edged Sabrina toward the coffee counter.

"Harold dropped her off at Nana's."

They both ordered creamy chocolate mochas. Laurin practically insisted that she pay. When the drinks were served, the masks came down; Sabrina felt reasonably comfortable because they were sitting side-by-side and not face-to-face.

"I guess I could figure out how to expand my website," Laurin said. "Put up pictures and descriptions, but why would anyone want to order online from me when they have a bigger choice from the big stores?"

"People still like to handle the merchandise, feel the textures of what they are buying. Look at the colors instead of seeing them on a screen. The screens don't always get those things right."

"You're doing online – how is that working out?"

"So-so. Most of them have actually already been in the shop, maybe asked me for help with a pattern, visited with some of the other knitters – and people who crochet, although I'm not much help with crochet and I never really got into needle-point."

"I don't have customers like that. I don't know what to do."

"And, I'm having a sidewalk sale." She realized that with each telling she was even deeper into commitment. This is really happening. Nothing to it but to do it.

"A sidewalk sale? How are you managing that?" Sabrina thought, of course Laurin gets it. Immediately. She's smart, a real lean-forward entrepreneur from way back. No questions about how or what to do. So simple, so clean. Laurin was helping Sabrina's confidence that the sidewalk sale was the idea she thought it was. It's not a lifeboat, Sabrina thought, it's a navigation chart.

"The permit clerk said as far as she knew there were no mandates against sidewalk sales. I'm having a three-day sale, Thursday, Friday and Saturday. I'm going to order extra inventory from my suppliers."

Laurin's mouth had fallen open. "Could I get a permit, too?"

"I don't know why not!" Sabrina thought Laurin was even thinner than she had been the day of the argument in the grocery store. Her eyes were not swollen, but dark-ringed.

"A sidewalk sale," Laurin mused and gazed at the ceiling as if she were seeing angels. She sipped the last of her mocha and slid off the stool. "I'll stop at City Hall on my way home. She paused to stare at Sabrina. "Are you feeling okay?"

"Yes," Sabrina said a little defensively. "Why?"

"You look a little pale. My husband's sister has the virus. He was with her about three weeks ago. He says he feels fine, no temperature or anything, but he's sweating it out. He won't go to any of the testing sites, but he can't evade the department testing." Laurin and Sabrina separated as they each selected a shopping cart.

Sabrina said, "I hope Irwin doesn't get it."

Laurin said, "You're a good friend. Stay safe." as she turned to shop.

Sabrina finished her shopping quickly. She looked for Laurin again, but only caught a glimpse of her at the rear of one of the aisles. One her way home, Sabrina noticed someone putting a sign for a Covid testing site in the Overlake Boulevard parkway. Impulsively, she turned the steering wheel and joined a short line of waiting vehicles in a bank parking lot. When she was next in line, she opened the window.

At her turn two women so heavily encumbered with personal protective equipment it was impossible to recognize them approached the car. While one of them prepared a nose swab, the other asked for pertinent information and her photo ID. The nose swab was uncomfortable, but quickly over with. One of the women advised her that she would receive a phone call with the results. "It could be several hours," the voice warned.

At home Sabrina made herself a cup of tea. Harold had brought the newspaper in from the driveway. Sabrina carried both the paper and the cup of tea to a sunlit window in the living room. Sabrina had not been a regular reader of the obituaries before the virus, but she noticed herself drifting there soon after the onset of the disease. Some obituaries listed a cause of death, many others gave a clue to the cause by the suggested memorials. A few openly cited Covid as the cause of death, and from some it could easily be imagined a lonely death in a nursing home facility.

Sabrina was still on the obituary pages when Nana called her. "Could you possibly come get Elsbeth before you go to the shop?"

"Is Elsbeth okay?" Unease filled Sabrina's thoughts.

"Elsbeth's fine. I want to go to a funeral this afternoon."

"A funeral? Whose?" Sabrina thought she had scanned all the notices and not found any whose name she recognized. Besides there were almost no funerals right now.

"Mr. Deakins. Harvey Deakins."

At first Sabrina couldn't find it, a very brief notice, divided at the bottom of one column and the top of the next, service at 1:30 pm. The listing of a service time seemed strange, since most of the other obituaries mentioned that services would be held at a later date.

"How do you know Mr. Deakins?"

"I don't. But he was a friend of my friend and I know she can't go. They were at the same nursing home," said Nana. "Somebody needs to be there. For him." She paused. "For her."

Nana's answer boggled Sabrina's mind. A friend of a friend? "Who is your friend?"

"Marjorie Dannefort. You might remember her. We were in the garden club together. She was very worried about Mr. Deakins. She thought he had died and then she found out they had moved him to a new room, and she thought he didn't have

Covid. And now he has died from something. She may not even know the way the place is operating. He lived in the assisted living where she lives. He only had a son who lives somewhere away. I haven't been able to talk to her for several days. If she even knows he's dead she wouldn't be able to go to any services, so I am going to go for her. I'll be able to tell her what happened, if the son was even able to come."

Sabrina thought her mother-in-law might be on the verge of tears. "I'll come get Elsbeth. I've just been to the grocery store – is there anything I can bring you?"

"No. I've ordered some postage stamps online. I can't think of anything else."

"You need stamps today? I have some."

"No. Thank you."

"I'll come to get Elsbeth in a few minutes."

"I keep meaning to tell you – I know it's slightly out-of-season, but I've been working on a pumpkin cushion, like a sofa cushion, not a round pumpkin."

Sabrina hoped that Elsbeth would be watching for her and would come bounding out of Nana's house. When Elsbeth did not appear she wearily pulled her mask up from her neck. She stayed just inside the door, keeping as much distance between herself and Nana as she could. "How's your neighbor, Carruthers? He still stopping over for morning coffee?"

"Oh, yes. He was real worried about his granddaughter coming to stay with him, but he's hardly seen her. She went over to the hospital the first day she was here and they hired her on the spot. She was gone early this morning, still hasn't unpacked her car."

"She's not a nurse, right?"

"No. Dayl said she is some kind of floor aide. At least it's started him downsizing to make room for when she does unload her car. He's been so reluctant to get rid of anything, particularly anything connected to Emmie."

"That's a blessing. Life goes forward. Elsbeth, come along now. Mom has a lot of work to do." She turned back to Nana. "I

79

thought you had helped him get rid of some of Emmie's things."

"Her coats. I talked him into giving all her coats to the Project Warmth coat drive. Took such a toll on him he couldn't do any more. I'm a good enough friend I don't push him."

"Elsbeth, aren't you ready yet?" In the car Sabrina pressed her palm against Elsbeth's forehead, but couldn't tell whether the warmth was from Elsbeth's head or her own hand. "I'm sorry, sweetie. I have to stop at the post office for more boxes and I can't leave you alone in the car. You'll have to come in with me. Be ready to pull up your mask." Online sales were great, might even be the salvation of the shop, but the shipping materials were quite expensive. She kept failing to call Logan Paper Goods to see if they might be able to supply cheaper boxes. She was pleased that a streetside parking spot opened up right in front of the post office. Fortunately, there was no waiting line. Elsbeth helped her carry some of the boxes out to the car. Definitely, get back to Logan's.

She hated to make Elsbeth walk to the shop, but she parked in the municipal lot more than a block away. Elsbeth helped her pull the trap-box back inside the shop. The trap-box was a heavy wooden container designed and built by Harold that let delivery companies deliver packages that arrived before her regular opening time of 11 am. Pulled back inside the shop, it served as a bench. Without a backward glance Elsbeth headed to the back of the store and padded chair in which she sometimes took a nap. "I hope you're not getting sick, Baby," Sabrina said and knew by a flick of her head that her daughter had heard her but did not appreciate being called a baby.

The trap-box yielded two packages. Yarn always had more bulk than weight: a box could feel almost empty and yet be full of delicious featherweight yarn. One was a box from a large yarn wholesaler, and the other, a big plastic envelope, had a Nebraska return address. Heart of the Mountain? In Nebraska? The yarn from the wholesaler was always predictable, glorious shades and hues, but dye lots that a knitter could always count on. Smaller artisan producers created awesome color shadings but usually in smaller quantities. Something available one season would be out of stock the next. Never enough to make an afghan, maybe barely enough to make a long-sleeve sweater, only sufficient for stunning hats and scarves and mittens.

Heart of the Mountain? That might be an interesting place to visit, or at least drive through on the way to some other vacation spot. A trip? Sabrina knew people who took a trip every summer like clockwork. A trip? Only if she could find someone reliable to run the shop in her absence. Only if lost sales because of the Pandemic didn't force her to shut the door entirely. Ironic. If she closed the shop she would have freedom to travel but no way to pay for it.

She opened the box and was pleased that the contents were exactly what she had asked for – nothing was on back order. She carefully cut open the big white plastic envelope. She gasped when four skeins of an enchanting multi-shaded navy blue that became a soft grey spilled out. She immediately thought of Chip Quinn. Chip was a closet knitter. On the rare times that he wandered into the shop he tried to leave the impression that he was running an errand for his wife. Sabrina arranged the four skeins as if they were falling out of the package and posted a picture on the shop Facebook page. If Chip happened to look, he'd probably come flying in to claim the precious yarn.

Elsbeth slept for a long time and when she woke up she was hungry. Sabrina took that for a good sign. If she were ill, she probably would not have an appetite. "Do you want to share a sandwich with me? I'll call the new deli down the street." When Sabrina made the call, the phone was answered by a woman.

"Jamma here, The Finest in the Caribbean. What delight can we prepare for you today?"

"You're Jamma? You were over in The Green, weren't you? I saw your sign that you were moving to Huron Street."

"Yes, and we did. We think we're going to be very happy here."

"Well, welcome to the business-hood. You have a lot of courage to start up in a new location during a Pandemic but this part of town seems to be staying busy."

"Fortunately, the governor thinks food service is an essential business. People have to eat. What would you like?"

"Oh, a ham and cheese sandwich . . ."

"A ham cutter. How about a couple of cookies?"

"Okay. A snickerdoodle and a brownie."

"How about a sunbutter and a hojarasca?"

A little bewildered but willing to try the new, Sabrina agreed. "Give me a call when it's ready and I'll come get it."

Sabrina's call had been answered by a woman; the call that the order was ready was from a man and it was a man who met Sabrina at the doorway of the deli.

"Hi," he said. He held out a brown paper bag. "From Jamma's Deli – The Finest of the Caribbean. A ham cutter with cheese and two cookies? And a special treat on the house – some Fry Jacks – you'll like these. I didn't realize you were on foot. I thought this was curbside."

"My shop's a couple of doors down. I'm the yarn lady."

"I'm Jamma's husband. Hello the Yarn Lady!" with a friendly smile. "Greg here. Lost my job and she needed help, but I'm a rookie at this. I may lose this job, too, if things don't pick up. Curbside customers don't quite make up for the loss of income."

"We're hurting, too. I've picked up a little online business, shipping orders out, but it takes a bit of time to get orders ready to ship, plus the expense of shipping materials. We're going to have a three-day sidewalk sale. People can shop even if we can't let them inside."

"A sidewalk sale? You got a permit for a sidewalk sale?"

"The permit clerk said no one had told her that she couldn't issue permits for sidewalk sales."

"It would sure help to get things jumpstarted on our street." Sabrina could tell he was considering the idea. "When were you thinking?"

Sabrina was sure telling a lot of people about something that she was pulling together on the fly. "Thursday, Friday, Saturday, two weeks from now."

"Hmmmm. A sidewalk sale? I'll talk it over with Jamma.

Maybe we can figure something out. Thanks for the tip. We might join you; two sales are better than none! Anything for some foot traffic." Wordlessly they agreed customers and foot traffic were desperately needed.

Elsbeth was perkier after the food. She viewed the Fry Jacks with suspicion, but ended up eating all of the delicious morsels that Sabrina hadn't been able to snatch away from her. "Maybe we can try to make them some time." Sabrina asked Elsbeth to help check the orders going out for shipment and to help print the invoice. When another delivery was dropped off at the front door, Sabrina let Elsbeth open the package. Sabrina was pleased to see the colors Mrs. Newquist was waiting for. She called Mrs. Newquist, who said it was too late in the day to drive into town, but she would try to come to town the next day.

Sabrina and Elsbeth were carrying the out-bound boxes for shipment into the post office lobby when the ad manager from the local newspaper called. "We hear you are having a sidewalk sale. You'll be needing an advertisement. How about a 2 x 6?"

With hope and enthusiasm Sabrina responded, "I think I'll take a 2 x 8," and then another thought occurred to her. She had told maybe a half a dozen people, so far: "How did you know?"

"The Caribbean deli down the street from you. Jamma sounded very excited," said the friendly voice on the line. "Of course we're delighted too. With so many businesses on lockdown, we're losing income like everybody. This town needs momentum. You may have found it."

Jamma, it turns out, hardly ever stands still.

NANA

Chapter Nine

Anna Harkins created a great scene at the funeral home. Except for a hearse at the side door, the parking lot was empty. Anna was the scene.

She hesitated at the entryway, not really sure if she could force herself to go inside. Over the years she had gone to many funeral services at McCandle & Evans, and it was the funeral home Hank had chosen for his services.

There was no one in the lobby, but a guest book for those attending to sign was on a podium outside the chapel. Anna noted that her signature would be the first, and she thought, maybe the only. She signed both her name and that of Marjorie Dannefort, and entered the chapel. That room, too, was empty. She walked down the center aisle and chose a seat in the second row. Left. The coffin was covered with an abundance of flowers. From a side area not visible to Anna came the sounds of an organ. She recognized the hymn as 'Love Divine . . . all loves excelling' . . . she could remember the words, could lightly hum the melody. She could tell that the music was not from a recording; she could hear the rustle of turning pages.

Silently, a tall man in a dark formal business suit with a black mask came down the center aisle and paused at the pew where Anna was sitting. He wore a puzzled frown; it seemed to Anna that he was trying to remember who she was. When he opened his mouth, he spoke softly. "Ma'am, this is not a public service . . ."

Nervously, Anna pulled her mask up from her throat. "It's for Harvey Deakins, isn't it?"

"Yes, you are correct. But because of the Pandemic, we are not holding public services, and I'll have to ask you to leave."

Suddenly, from a side door, a man focusing a video camera emerged. "Let her stay. Please." The man was nicely dressed, but in a travel jacket, not formal attire. He held the camera on Anna and the funeral home representative. "I'm sure my father would have appreciated her presence." The funeral home representative took a few steps backward. The man with the camera pushed a button, transferred the camera to his left hand and offered his right to Anna. "I'm Raymond Deakins. Harvey Deakins was my father. Thank you for coming. How did you know my Dad?"

"I never met him," Anna admitted, "but he was a very good friend of a very good friend of mine," Anna clarified. "A very good friend of a best friend."

"Marjorie Dannefort?" the funeral home representative asked. "She signed the guest book, but I do not see her . . . is she in the ladies room?"

"She's in the nursing home where Mr. Deakins lived." Anna did not say that she suspected that Marjorie might not even know as yet of Mr. Deakins' death. "She was not able to come today, so I came for her. I signed her in. I will be able to tell her all about the services."

"They let you visit her?" blurted Raymond.

"No, not in person. We talk on the telephone. When the phones are working."

Raymond lifted his right arm with the camera and moved away from Anna. An elderly woman was assisting an older man, garbed in clerical attire, make his way to the front of the chapel. Fingers grasping both sides of the podium, his voice feeble with age, the minister offered a beginning prayer. Raymond took the nearest place to sit and kept the camera focused on the cleric.

As the man continued to read passages from a Bible in front of him, it was obvious to Anna that the older minister had been the vicar at the church Mr. Deakins had attended in his younger days. The old vicar related memories, many old memories, of Mr. Deakins and how he had provided for his family and served the church through a long lifetime. Raymond recorded every word with his video camera.

At the end of the vicar's final benediction two younger men in jeans and flannel shirts appeared to roll the coffin out to the waiting hearse. Anna noticed that Raymond did not film the two men in work clothing. She went out to the parking lot and drove her car into what would have been a line behind the hearse. Raymond came over to the passenger side of her car; Anna rolled down the window.

"You're going to the cemetery?" Raymond asked.

Anna didn't tell Raymond that Hank Sr. was buried at Greenhaven Cemetery. "Yes, I'm going."

"May I ride with you?"

"Yes. Of course." No hesitation. Company would be better for her too. Anna pulled up her Covid mask and leaned over to move a couple of small items off of the passenger seat. "Give me a minute."

Raymond stepped away to tell the funeral home people that he would not be riding in the hearse. Anna had the passenger area mostly cleared; Raymond opened the door.

"My grandmother always had the passenger seat loaded with her projects. You didn't know her either? Edith Deakins?"

"I don't know that I did, but Overlake didn't used to be as big as it is now. In the old days people pretty much knew everybody, by sight anyway, even if they didn't know their name. Now Overlake is just a suburb of Metropole." The hearse began to move; Anna eased behind it; only two vehicles, there was no police escort.

"I live in Chicago. I've gotten back for visits . . . when I can. I didn't know Dad was in such poor condition until the nursing home called me, but they said that because of the Pandemic they couldn't even let me in the building. Long time ago, maybe a year and a half ago, Dad and I talked about what kind of a service he wanted to have. He wanted the old vicar from his church. I even contacted the vicar, who said he would consider it an honor. I didn't know until this morning that the vicar had suffered a stroke – his wife told me."

"It was good of him to come – obviously quite an effort for him. He must have a great deal of . . . ", she thought respect but found herself saying " . . . love for your father. His remarks were meaningful."

" . . . and for his wife, too. Dad would have remembered her also. Well, when the nursing home told me there was no way I could get there in time, and I wouldn't be allowed to see him anyway . . . ," his voice faltered and he cleared his throat ". . . I asked them to tell him that his service was going to be exactly the way he planned it. I hope they told him. He must have been lonely . . . it must be awful to die alone . . ."

Anna couldn't look at Raymond; she was certain he was crying. Hank Sr.'s passing was hard enough, before Covid.

"I brought my camera . . . I had the feeling I was making a video I could show to Dad some day. Crazy."

Anna also was near tears. She kept her eyes on the hearse in front of her. She was sorry she had to be here and very glad she had come. She, too, had experienced the same kind of time warp as Raymond when she somehow thought she could talk directly with Hank, when all the rest of the world knew him to be dead.

At the graveside the hearse was met by the same two young men in jeans and flannel shirts who helped guide the coffin onto the platform that would lower it to rest. The vicar had not followed the cortege to the cemetery. The funeral home representative who had driven the hearse had a few remarks to be read from a page of notes. Raymond kissed the palm of his hand and laid it on the coffin for a few seconds. Then with the same hand he offered a handshake to Anna. "This good man is going to take me to the airport. Thank you again for coming. Tell your friend, Dad's friend, Marjorie, that after all the Pandemic madness is over, I'll try to come to see her, show her the video. The three of us can visit the cemetery together."

Despite all the warnings, despite the fact that Raymond was standing closer than the six-foot social distance requirement, despite that they were all well-masked, Anna wrapped her arms as best she could around Raymond's body and gave him a real hug, for Raymond, for Marjorie, and Edith, and for Hank Sr. After a moment of surprise, he returned the hug.

Anna delayed her departure until the hearse could no longer be seen and then drove to the location of Hank's grave. She walked over to the double tombstone, his name and hers, with empty space left for the final date of her existence. She noted with pleasure that despite the regular maintenance of the grounds, the little sprig of vinca she had planted had established some very stubborn roots. The deep green leaves, the happy little "surprise" blooms up from under.

Leaving the cemetery, Anna did not head for home; she had no clear direction, only that it felt good to be behind the wheel of a car again. She rarely drove anymore, even less with Covid. She stayed off the Interstate, but she knew the alternate slower roadways. The last time she renewed her driver's license, she had asked her optometrist to fill out the vision form. The optometrist had backed up her belief that her peripheral vision was still good. She was not quite as familiar with Overlake as Hank had been, but she would never get lost. Anna turned toward Lakeshore, the loveliest drive in Overlake, a scenic delight that curved around the shores of Lake Palmer.

Retiring as superintendent of the Overlake Water Department, Hank Sr. had known every boulevard, street, avenue, road, drive, alley and pathway in Overlake. Except for a few short summers when he worked at a grocery store, Hank's entire career had been with the Overlake Water Department. For someone without a college degree, the water department had been a ladder to success. Often in the early years Hank had come home with his shoes and clothing covered with mud because he had been digging down in the trenches. Why did it always seem like the lines broke on the worst weather days? Burning hot. Blistering cold. Never easy. As he advanced, the dirty work was done by the newer employees but Hank Sr., she remembered proudly, never shied from handwork. Or hard work. And he passed that on to Harold.

Hank Sr. had brought Dayl into the water department. Dayl had a good job with a credit card company, but lost his position during a painful RIF – reduction in force. Hank Sr. took him on as a temporary hire until he could find another job, but Dayl took the challenge, earned a starting role and stayed. Became superintendent himself after Hank retired, although it was only a short time until Dayl retired as well.

The end of Lakeshore led right into The Green. In the early years of their marriage, Anna had been employed by the same grocery store where Hank Sr. had worked, choosing to be on deck for an early shift, so she could be at home when school was dismissed. She had to fill in for some weekend hours occasionally, but the upside was that she could get compensatory time off during the weekday. And it sure helped the grocery bill.

With dismay, the employees watched as a big grocery store chain tore down every building in an entire nearby block, erected a building the size of a half-block and opened a grocery emporium complete with a pharmacy, a deli section and an upscale corner restaurant. Within a month of the grand opening of the new behemoth, the little neighborhood grocery closed its doors. Mom and Pop took retirement. Earlier than they had intended but facts were, are, fact. With the owners' strong recommendations the employees looked for other jobs, but none of them applied at the new store. The owners moved to South Texas and after years of standing empty, the building became an antique boutique.

Hank Sr. had been diligent about keeping his professional credentials up to date, but he deeply regretted not being able to get a college degree. From the time Harold entered kindergarten Hank Sr. had talked college.

For two years Harold dutifully went to junior college. For his junior year, Harold went off to university, where he met a timid, lost freshman on the first day. An unexpected cold snap in mid-October found him without appropriate weather gear; overnight, Sabrina knit him a warm cap. Harold stuck it out, finished the fall semester, but when he came home he told his mother that he was looking for a job. Arney Faulkner, starting a vending machine company, took Harold on as a probation. Harold and Sabrina were married when Sabrina finished that spring semester. Neither finished college.

Not finishing college bothered Hank Sr. He never mentioned it to Harold or Sabrina. But Nana knew it was a burr under his saddle. But it never bothered Nana. They were so good for each other. And then so good for their children. And, she thought to herself, they were accomplishing so much so well without the actual degrees. Nana found herself hoping that college had taught both of them just enough to understand what a good life they were building. Besides, where would either of them find the time?

— § —

Dayl Carruthers waited ten minutes before crossing the driveway to Anna's house. "I haven't had my morning coffee," he complained. "Good grief, girl, it's almost suppertime."

"Have you forgotten how to make your own coffee?" Anna teased him. She switched on the oven and moved to the counter; she was ready for a cup of coffee herself. She didn't mention the services or burial for Mr. Deakins; Dayl's Emmie also was buried at Greenhaven Cemetery. "How is the granddaughter?"

"I've hardly seen her. I think she has a new boyfriend."

"That seemed to be an astute observation for an old guy. She just got here!" Anna used scissors to cut open a packet of frozen cookie dough and put four clumps of dough on a baking sheet. With her leg she brushed two cats out of the way and opened the oven door.

"I know. But I overheard her talking to her college roommate. It seems to be maybe someone she met at the hospital. Maybe a doctor. Who knows?"

"Maybe that's why you aren't seeing much of her. It may not be your cooking after all." Anna pushed a mug of hot fresh coffee over towards Dayl with a smile.

"I don't think she's actually met this guy. She's plotting for some way to run into him." Dayl took a tentative sip of coffee, testing it for temperature. And he protested, "There's nothing wrong with my cooking."

"What's Tressa doing at the hospital?"

"As far as I can figure out, she's shadowing someone to train into their systems. I'm sure she's qualified enough and the hospital is desperate for help. They seem overrun. Maybe I should get a job too."

"It could be a cure for loneliness."

"I thought she was supposed to be doing online lessons like Nathan, but I don't think she has even touched her laptop. She hasn't unloaded her car, either. She washes her uniform – her scrubs – every night because there is such a shortage of everything. They gave her one, maybe two sets, with someone else's name on them." Dayl lifted his head and looked at the oven hopefully.

Anna jumped up. "Oh, dear, by the time you can smell them they're almost overbaked." She pulled the baking sheet from the oven and set two cookies before Dayl. "Wait a minute. They'll burn your mouth!"

Outside the window the streetlamps flashed on. Anna turned on the light over the kitchen table and picked up her knitting.

"Is that another of your Chameleon scarves?"

"No." Anna held the work up. "I'm trying to make a sort of a round flat pumpkin."

"But Hallowe'en is over."

"For next year. I have in mind a sort of a sofa pillow. I haven't decided whether I want to put on eyes and a mouth or not."

"Emmie's pumpkin pies were always some of my favorites. I'm sorry but I bought the one I brought over."

"I remember Emmie's. They were so good. Emmie sometimes made an extra pie for Hank Sr. and me. They were always a highlight." The quiet hung until Anna thought to ask, "When will Tressa be home from the hospital?"

"Not for another few hours, not until they get everyone settled down for the night. Seems like she is coming in just after nine or so."

"You might as well stay here and have supper with me. It won't be anything fancy."

"Danged if I won't. I'd be happy with leftovers. Thank you for the invitation. What can I do to help?"

"Not a thing." Anna put her knitting back inside her kit which was labeled STAY CALM AND KEEP KNITTING.

They were almost finished with a simple meal of grilled cheese sandwiches and onion soup when Anna's land line telephone rang.

"Mom?"

"Yes." Anna knew immediately it was Harold who was calling. He knew he should speak first because Anna would not answer until she recognized the voice. Anna could hear someone sobbing in the background. She pressed the speaker button.

"We've got some bad news here. Sabrina has tested positive and will have to quarantine. Elsbeth will have to quarantine, too. Sabrina has some symptoms, but I'm not sure about Elsbeth."

"Oh, dear, I'm truly sorry about that."

"You can probably hear her crying. She was with her friend Laurin this morning. She just called Laurin to tell her about testing positive. She's afraid she's infected Laurin as well."

"She must be crushed. It's pretty rare to hear that girl cry.

What can I do?"

"Well, for one thing, can Nathan come to stay at your house? I'm having him pack a bag right now."

"Of course. Have him bring his schoolbooks with him. And computer."

Harold confirmed his mother's suspicions with his next remark, his voice lowered. "Sabrina's about in hysterics. Upset about having to totally close the store. I can't help her. We – the vending company – is having the strangest kind of experiences. One day we have more vending machine problems than we can handle, more than we can possibly get done and the next day it's a desert. The hospital had an emergency removal to clear the way for the parking lot conversion and two days later they want more machines installed in the cafeteria."

"Sounds like no one person knows what's going on."

"This Pandemic confuses everything." The sound of the sobbing had changed as if Sabrina had gone to another part of the house.

"Didn't Sabrina have someone lined up as a substitute? That woman who was available part-time? What was her name?" Anna asked.

"She's got the virus. All her three kids too. Would any of your knitting friends be able to work a few days? I can be there to help between service calls."

"They've all got other commitments. One of them is taking care of an invalid husband – he was ill before the Pandemic. One of them baby-sits her grandchildren so her daughter can work. I can't think of a single person who could run the knit shop for a few days."

"What about me?" Dayl shouted, loud enough to be heard by Harold on the other end of the line.

After a pause and considering the late hour at his mother's house, Harold asked, "Who was that?"

"Dayl, my neighbor, Dayl Carruthers. You know Dayl. I don't know that he knows anything about the knitting business."

"I know how to answer the phone," Dayl shouted again. "I

know how to count money. And, I'm available. Quite available. You don't even have to pay me, but I may ask for a recommendation when Sabrina gets back on deck."

"I know a little about the business. I might be able to get by if you got stuck on something." Harold shouted.

Anna handed the telephone to Dayl. "Maybe you two should be the ones on the phone," Anna said. "Get me out of the shouting."

Harold asked "Would you really? Could you really?"

Dayl reassured Harold that he would and he could. How hard could it be? How much is there to selling yarn?

"I'm bringing Nathan over in a few minutes. If you don't mind hanging around, I can bring you the key. We can talk."

"That'll be fine. I haven't had my dessert yet," Dayl said and then ducked as Anna made a swipe at him with a tea towel. They both heard Harold yell "Sabrina . . . " as he ended the call.

Twenty minutes later Harold pulled into his mother's driveway and strode into her kitchen. Anna resisted the impulse to hug him. She'd had too many hugs already for one day. Dayl pulled his mask up from this throat and stood with his back to the counter. Anna's glance swept the room: three adults wearing masks, as much social distancing as the space would allow. Harold laid a key on the table and drew back; Dayl moved forward to pick up the key.

"How are you going to manage?" Anna asked her son.

"I'm going to be staying in the basement. I can't leave them totally alone. I think it will work out. I've got all of our camping gear." He paused, "Indoor camping. Who'da thunk?" He turned to face Dayl. "Thanks for being willing to fill in at the store. Sabrina will write out some instructions and I will bring them to the store. We'll have to figure out how to pay you. This Pandemic gets stranger every day."

From her position near the door to the dining room, Anna was trying to peer outside. "Where's Nathan? I thought you were bringing Nathan?"

Harold also tried to peer outside. "Where'd he go? Did he already get past us?"

Dayl had the best view through the window over the counter. "Nathan's out in the driveway. He's talking to Tressa, my grand-daughter," he said.

Harold mumbled, 'Teenager, huh.'

DAYL

Chapter Ten

t 10:50 am Dayl parked his car in the municipal parking lot and crossed the street to the knit shop.

Even though he had driven past many times before, he had never looked in the window. As he neared the door, Dayl looked at the shop. The window was bright. Not from light but from color. It was a rainbow, no, more a kaleidoscope. Colors, and yarns, and projects, and clothes. But not disorganized or too much. Neat, attractive, inviting. Sabrina's window suggested a good thing. And for a casual passerby who had never knit anything her or his whole life, Sabrina's window could at least make them curious.

Dayl knew that Anna's daughter-in-law and family ran the shop, but what did he know about yarns – besides telling a few – would fill a very short book. "I've never even been in the store and here I think I can help run it. In a Pandemic." He smiled wryly inside, maybe the only plus to the Pandemic was that the limited customer traffic would be light enough that he'd have time to learn what he needed to know to be useful. Before he needed it. What was that old saw, 'Fake it until . . .' He also thought about how proud he was that Tressa had done the same thing: she stepped right up to help when the call came. In a way she had encouraged him.

As he neared the shop Dayl noticed a man carrying something in both hands emerge from Jamma's Finest of the Caribbean Deli. At the present trajectory they would arrive at the knit shop door at the same time. Key in hand, Dayl slowed his footsteps. So did the other man.

The man made a slight upward motion with the things he was carrying. "Compliments of Jamma, the Finest of the Caribbean," he said with a backward tip of his head. "She's really excited about the sidewalk sales Sabrina told us about. It sounds like a super idea to get the economy moving along. She's sent over a some fresh pastafrolas – I think they are quince -- and one of her latte specials."

"Obviously I'm not Sabrina," Dayl replied. "But I do enjoy my morning coffee. Usually I'm just plain old coffee and cream, but I'm willing to try a latte. It might become a habit." Dayl set the key in the door lock. "But I'm in the dark about any sidewalk sales."

"Sabrina's planning a three-day sidewalk sale, said the permit clerk was issuing permits because there were no Covid restrictions against it," the man continued.

"I hadn't heard that. There may be a problem, though." Dayl pushed the door open and had his first look inside the shop. "Sabrina's tested positive. She and her daughter are both in quarantine." He motioned for the man to set the food items on a small table at the front of the store. "I know nothing about running a yarn store. I've just volunteered to be on the premises and to do what I can," Dayl added. "I'm a friend of the family." He wasn't really sure what he was, if anything, to Anna.

The man laughed. "Nothing like learning on the job. I'm Greg, Jamma's husband. I used to work for a financial services company, but I'm on furlough now. I'm learning fast about the deli business. I knew my wife was good, but up close she's even better. And expects a lot from her help." He laughed, "And no special treatment for the husband!" He patted his stomach. "It helps that I have a good appetite. I guess I'm training for barista."

Dayl started to offer a handshake and then they both did a quick back away. Greg offered an elbow bump, to which Dayl awkwardly responded. "Old dogs learning new tricks. Ha! Tell Jamma thanks for the food. I'll have to stop in."

"Eating," Greg pronounced. "You know it's habit-forming. I may never go back to my old job."

Both men were startled by a voice at the rear of the store. "73, good buddy. I'm destinated. Catch you down the road. KDØRVQO. Out." Harold shut the back door and made his way to the front. "Here's the instructions from Sabrina . . ." He paused at the sight of Greg. "Sorry, didn't realize you had a customer already."

"Not a customer. This is Greg from the Caribbean Deli a couple of doors down. He brought life-saving rations." To Greg, Dayl explained. "This is Harold Harkins, Sabrina's husband. He works for a vending machine company, but who knows? By tomorrow he may be a journeyman yarnster, too."

Sabrina's instructions covered three typed sheets. Dayl recognized good business habit when he saw them. This would be a big help catching on.

Harold waved an acknowledgment to Greg, on his way out the door, and laid the papers on the table next to the food bag. "These are probably self-explanatory. I'd try to go over them with you, but I do at the moment have a job and the vending machines at the Country Mall are out of whack. Happens every time some kid tries to use one of those game tokens. You wouldn't believe what I've taken out of vending machines." As Harold went out the back door the shop phone rang. Dayl was wondering, for a moment, what people put into vending machines. That Harold did take out. But the phone was beckoning before he gave it too much thought.

"Hello? Mr. Carruthers?" Dayl recognized Sabrina's voice from their many driveway visits at Anna's.

"Good morning, Sabrina. Its 'Dayl' if I am going to work here."

"It's just so good of you to help run the shop."

"Well, I'm sorry that you need me, but I'm glad to help.

You've gotta beat this thing."

"I'm working on it. But the truth is I am worried about the kids. And Harold. Has he been by there yet?"

"Yea, he just left. He came in from the back. Do you want me to see if I can catch him?"

"No. It's you I need to talk to. Did I put in my instructions something about Mrs. Newquist?"

"I don't know. I haven't had time to read them. And do call me Dayl. You've known me long enough."

"Yes, Dayl. Thank you. Mrs. Newquist will probably be coming in for some special yarn that I had ordered for her. It's already in a little bag under the cash register."

"I'll look for it. Wait a minute. There's a FedEx delivery guy at the door." Dayl set the phone down and headed for the door, but before he could get there the FedEx guy dropped a box at the door and waved a good-bye. Dayl decided there was something wrong with the picture; he delayed picking up the phone and continued to watch the FedEx guy get back in the truck.

With the phone in his hand again, he remarked to Sabrina, "I think your FedEx guy is a girl."

Sabrina chuckled. 'Sometimes that's the case. They're kind of disguised by the uniform." She was overcome with a cough. "I'll let you go to read the instructions. Call me if you have any questions."

"Will do. The deli down the street sent some little Caribbean fruit pies and a latte, presumably for you, but I won't let them go to waste."

"Good thinking." Sabrina said 'Thank You' enough times before getting off the phone it embarrassed Dayl.

A tap on the back door made Dayl think that Harold had returned. Harold did not appear, however, and at another knock Dayl went back through the short hallway to investigate. He opened the door to a medium height young man – to Dayl almost everyone who had not reached the age of retirement was young – with a light ginger moustache and beard. The young man looked bewildered. "Sabrina?"

"No. She tested positive ... " he didn't need to say for what, " ... and is starting quarantine. I'm filling in. How can I help you?" He stepped back with an inviting gesture.

"Sabrina got some unusual yarn in. I haven't been able to come in for several days – I was on quarantine too. I hope I didn't give it to her. Sabrina put a note online. She didn't say she was holding it for me, but she sort of implied that I might want to have a look-see."

"Come on in and take a look. Give me time to read the instructions she sent for my first day. I'll see if we can find it." Dayl opened the box from Jamma's deli that Greg had brought. "Have a fruit thing. I forget what they're called." Absently, Dayl took one of the four pastafloras from the box and began to read Sabrina's instructions. He found nothing except two lines that read: Chip Quinn may come in to look at some navy yarn from Heart of the Mountain. He looked at the young man. "Are you Chip Quinn?"

"That would be me." Chip was poking around in the bundles under the cash register. "Here it is. Heart of the Mountain. That's the new one." He shook four skeins of a variegated and quite luxuriant navy-grey yarn onto the table, then took one of the skeins into his hands for a closer examination. Carefully, he read the label, then offered the skein to Dayl. "It's 100 percent alpaca. Sensational how they did the dyeing. But there is no needle size recommended. What do you think? About a four or a five?"

Dayl turned the skein and noticed the number five under the symbol of two crossed knitting needles. "Five ought to do it." He had no idea what the '5' meant but it made sense in answer to Chip's question. Dayl didn't really know, yet, that knitting needles even had sizes. Were they like drill bits? Or European shoes? He knew he was on a crash course to find out.

"Only four skeins." Chip sounded disappointed. "My . . . wife . . . has been making shawls for the aunts, only one more to go, and she would love the colors, but I need more than four skeins – does the label have the number of meters?" Chip was wandering past the shelves of other yarns.

Again Dayl looked at the label. "Looks like 230 meters. Dayl knew the difference between a yard and a meter, but no idea how much yardage – or meterage, was there such a word? – might be needed to make a shawl. When Emmie talked about quilting it was always in quarters and inches and feet. She even talked about fat quarters.

"What is the price on these. Probably pretty high?"

"I don't know," Dayl stated. "I don't find it in the instructions. I'll see if I can get Sabrina." He picked up the shop phone.

While he waited, Chip browsed the shelves. He put two balls of glowing orange on the table. "Some of my hunting neighbors needed orange boot toppers this hunting season." He added a skein of soft grey alpaca.

"Orange boot toppers," Dayl said thoughtfully. "I have some neighbors who are out every hunting season . . . "

"They're easy to make. You don't even need a pattern. And if you really want them to look professional you use the Kitchener bind-off."

"Kitchener . . ." Dayl repeated, thinking it sounded like a sneeze. He said it again, fascinated with the resemblance. Of course the knitting tie was associated with the British military hero, Lord Kitchener. What connection Lord Kitchener might have with knitting was anybody's guess.

Sabrina called back with the price of $29.85 per skein, which Dayl thought was extremely pricey, but what did he really know about yarns? Apparently knitting was an expensive hobby, but weren't most hobbies? He had never bothered to ask how much money Emmie spent on quilting supplies. Chip readily paid the price and seemed to think he was getting a bargain. Dayl escorted Chip to the back door, and was surprised when Chip asked him a question. 'What is your current project?"

"Me? I'm not a knitter."

"But I thought . . . you're running the yarn store for Sabrina?" Chip swallowed hard. "Actually, I'm not a knitter either. I'm just running errands for my wife." He pushed the back door open. "She's the craft person in the family."

Curious, Dayl thought, as he closed the door. He wondered what he had said that caused Chip to think he was a knitter. He picked up the cardboard coffee mug with the latte. The coffee was lukewarm by now; he wandered to the back room, certain he would find a microwave. He carried Sabrina's sheets of instructions with him as he went. One of the first sentences his eyes lit on were directions for finding the microwave. She is good crossed Dayl's mind.

Sipping his warmed-over coffee he tried to slowly go over Sabrina's instructions. Nothing that seemed too difficult. Belatedly, he remembered the box the FedEx guy – or gal – had left at the front door and went to pick it up. When he opened the box the colors were mesmerizing – if he were a knitter, what could he make of these? Something more than boot toppers. He looked toward the back hallway – if Chip Quinn were still here, he would be one to ask.

Dayl called Sabrina, who asked for the sender and the invoice number. Sabrina said the incoming yarns should be entered in inventory, but she wasn't sure she could coach him how to do it over the phone.

"We could try," Dayl proposed. "I do my banking online."

"Okay. Pull out the computer with the sticker on it of the Overlake Chamber of Commerce." It took them a half-hour to get the new yarns entered in inventory and when they were almost finished another box arrived via UPS. "While we're at it we might as well keep going. Would that be okay with you?"

"Well, I think I am catching on now. Let's go for it." Dayl was longing for a second cup of coffee. "I do see that everything we put in inventory will eventually come out again."

"That's the goal. If it doesn't, it has to be marked down for sale. Can I hire you to help me with the sidewalk sale, if I ever get out of quarantine?"

"Greg, from the Deli, mentioned you're thinking about a sidewalk sale. When?"

"I have a permit for a three-day sale two weeks from now."

"Two weeks from now!?" He was trying to remember what

all of the newspeople were saying about how long for quarantine. And doing some quick calculations. "You'll just be clearing quarantine if you … ," he paused, "You know, it doesn't go … "

"Full Covid," she cut him off.

"Yea, full Covid." He was suddenly uncomfortable.

"I find myself saying little prayers pretty much all day right now." She made her commitment aloud, not so much for Dayl to hear but to set down a marker, to plant her flag, "I will be there. I will make the sidewalk sale. Covid isn't going to get me."

Dayl believed her. Somehow. But he didn't want to dwell on the Covid. Sabrina, and she'd said her daughter too, being touched by Covid was as close as he had been to anyone who was being afflicted. He wasn't really that comfortable with Tressa working at the hospital, but she assured him that every precaution was being taken and that she was not anywhere near the Covid wing. The staff was already fully vaccinated and vaccination clinics were rolling out through the community. Tressa had already gotten her first shot, as medical staff, and had even signed Dayl up for his vaccines.

"I'll be glad to help with the sidewalk sale but I can't do that alone – without you, or Harold, or … ," he didn't want to missend the wrong message, "Anna."

"Dayl, I know it is a lot to ask, but if you can just help me hang on through the planning and getting things ready, we'll have a great plan and a good team … "

He interrupted, "A great team and a good plan … " He was all in.

She said, "Yea, a great team and a good plan by the time we get to the sale."

"You really think I can convince anyone that an old guy like me knows anything about yarns?"

"Hey, there are guys who are knitters."

"I don't know. But I think I met one today."

"Oh, Chip? He came in by the back door, didn't he? He's afraid someone will see him. He was okay with the price?"

"Yes. He was delighted. He said he hadn't been in because he was in quarantine. But when he left he tried to tell me he was getting the yarn for his wife."

"Yes, that's his line. He doesn't want anyone to know he is a knitter. That's why he's never entered anything in the county fair. I'm sure he could have won some prizes. He's pretty good for a man." Neither of them gave any thought to lives full of unfair gender comparisons. Sabrina continued, "By the way, has Mrs. Newquist come in?"

"Not yet."

"That's strange. I thought she'd meet you at the door . . ."

Before turning to new business, Dayl thought it best to clear the deck with honesty. "I guess I should admit that between Chip and myself, we already finished the goodies sent to you from the Caribbean Deli."

"Oh, that's wonderful. They are going to be a nice neighbor. If they don't make us all fat! What was the occasion?"

"They're grateful about the sidewalk sales idea. Greg, I think he said Greg, said he was getting their permit today."

"Seems like people may be getting on board. The paper has already called. This may turn out to be something bigger than I expected."

"I think people are just excited about finding something to do," Dayl offered. "I know the feeling. You can only take some things for so long and then you need to do something to try to change things, hopefully for the better."

"Maybe that's the ticket," agreed Sabrina. "Let's do something," Sabrina added. "I need to send you some shipping orders for online sales. Maybe you can get them all organized and I will try to get Harold to go by the post office and bring you some boxes. If you can't find some of the items, call me because I can pretty well remember where everything is."

"Will do, Boss." He could tell that Sabrina was getting tired. It was a long talk.

—§—

Dayl was on his knees looking in the shelves for RoanRed Superwash when he was startled by an urgent knocking on the door. Turning the key to open the door he was preparing to ask a visibly upset young woman how he could help her.

Laurin McCurnin pushed past Dayl to call Sabrina's name. "Sabrina? Where are you?" She reached the back room before Dayl could turn around. "Sabrina? What do you mean about canceling the sidewalk sale? I've already ordered some extra inventory. Sabrina?"

"Sabrina's at home – in quarantine –"

Laurin moved back into the center of the main sales room. "She called me. Left a message. She's at home?"

"She tested positive. I'm sort of filling in temporarily. And if she's canceling the sidewalk sale she hasn't told me. She just asked me if I could help. Two weekends from now. We are Green-Light Go as far as I know."

Laurin brightened, then sat down limply in one of the straight-back chairs. "Maybe I misunderstood."

Dayl took a guess. "Maybe she was thinking we'd need to change the date to past her quarantine."

Laurin sighed. "I think you may be right. We're all so on edge, not knowing what's going to happen next." Tears began to well in her eyes. "All my life, growing up, my dream was always to have my own fashion store. Now I'm fighting like hell, sorry, heck and the stupid Pandemic is going to take it all away. Sabrina is so solid. The sidewalk sale feels like a life-raft. You know? We need hope. We need a plan. A Sidewalk Sale is a great plan."

Dayl wanted to pat her shoulder, as he had done when Emmie was upset, but he was wary of breaking the six-foot social distancing protocol. He looked around frantically for a box of facial tissue; he was sure he had seen an open box somewhere in the shop.

"We're all going to get through this thing. A year from now it will all be nothing but a painful memory," he said with a conviction he didn't have. "I don't think that there will be a change in the sale date." He spotted the facial tissues just as the telephone rang. He managed to get the tissues on the table in front of Laurin before he picked up the phone. "Knit shop."

"Sabrina?"

"No, this is Dayl. Sabrina isn't here today. How can we help you?"

"I was coming in today to pick up an order, but my car is in the repair shop and I've just been told that I won't get it back for several days."

"What is your address – I'm sure we can deliver your order to you."

"I don't live in town."

"You live close enough to drive to the shop. I'm sure we can find your house." He had offered, he wasn't sure why, before thinking it all the way through. Dayl realized that he really was 'all in'.

While Dayl was talking, Laurin quietly rose from her chair, waved a good-bye, smiling now, and was gone.

— § —

Dayl looked at the clock on the wall, a large custom-made device with knitting needles for hands. He was surprised at how fast the day was passing. Harold had not brought boxes from the post office, but Dayl was sure there were enough used boxes that could be recycled. Scrounging around in the back room Dayl found boxes to fit the size of each outgoing shipment. Where the shipping labels didn't cover the logos of the previous user Dayl generously applied brown shipping tape.

A truck as big as the shop window pulled against the curb, blocking Dayl's view of the street. Logan's Paper Goods. A driver emerged, looked doubtfully at the front of the store. He leaned on the glass of the window and cupped his hands to get a better look into the store. Dayl gave him a wave and went to open the door.

The driver opened the rear door of the truck, gathered up

numerous items and came through the shop door with an arm-load of cardboard boxes. Dayl recognized the driver as Captain Logan himself, from the days when they both had been involved in scouts.

"Sabrina not here?"

"Not here. She's at home in quarantine, to her dismay."

Captain Logan stopped to face Dayl. "That's too bad. How's she feeling? Can I give her a call? Jamma, the Caribbean Deli lady said something about sidewalk sales. Told me to talk to Sabrina."

"You have her number?"

"I'm sure it's in our database." Captain Logan shuffled his feet. "I want to talk to her about a couple of things. The other day she told me I should put out a sign with daily specials, tell people that we are open to the public. She said we looked like a warehouse. I've been doing what she said, and we've had a nice uptick in sales." He looked toward the front window. "Does she advertise that way?"

"I expect she does. I'm just a temporary fill-in while she's in quarantine. Don't ask me what I know about knitting."

Captain Logan tilted his head for a better look at Dayl. "Are you Sabrina's father?"

"No, she's my neighbor's daughter-in-law. Did you ever know Hank Harkins, the water superintendent?"

"Yes, I did. He's been gone a few years."

"His son, Harold, married Sabrina, and I guess they probably own the shop together. Harold works for Overlake Vending."

"I knew that. Small world." Captain Logan moved toward the door. "Gone crazy. Has us all wondering what the new normal will be."

Dayl waved him out the door. "Call Sabrina. She'll give you the rundown on sidewalk sales. She sure has a business mind."

Dayl didn't quite get lost on his way to Louise Newquist's house. Given the distance, he had second thoughts about offering a free delivery, but here he was. It was as Mrs. Newquist had said, third house from the corner and the porch lights were on.

He was sure he could see the figure of a woman standing on the other side of a storm door.

The woman motioned for Dayl to leave the package on the edge of the porch at the top of the short flight of stairs. Dayl gave her a nod of agreement. As he turned to leave she opened the door and called out with a thank-you. "You don't know how much I appreciate this."

He thought to say, 'cause he thought Sabrina might, "Sometime down the line you'll have to show us your work."

The woman hesitated. "Well . . . maybe."

"Don't be shy," Dayl called back. "I'm sure Sabrina would be interested."

— § —

Dayl was almost home before he remembered it had been his intention to go to the grocery store. There was little to eat besides beans in either the cabinets or the refrigerator. He decided he would wait until Tressa came home and order a pizza delivery. He didn't feel comfortable ordering beforehand because he had no idea what kind of pizza his granddaughter might prefer. Kids, the things they eat nowadays anyway. In haste, and alone, he headed for his computer – he had a certain type of programming he wanted to watch on YouTube.

It didn't take long after Dayl figured out how to 'Search'. Men. Learn. Knit. Beginner. He was surprised how many results popped back. And how quickly. He sampled a few. It didn't take long to find one he could relate to: "Sgt. Knitman teaches Men to Knit".

First she wasn't actually a Sargent – she was a retired U.S. Army Colonel. And her real name was obviously not "Knitman". But she could teach. She clearly had been in front of a lot of people teaching in the Army. And she was a little bit funny too.

"Get your needles at the Ready, Men." Dayl noticed that the word 'Ready' was displayed along the bottom of the screen as she talked. "Go with your #8s. Only one needle is used to start cast on. Hold it in whichever hand feels best. This will be your starting hand. But by the time you've been knitting for a while, you will think you are ambidextrous." Some trick that would be thought Dayl, trying to keep up.

"Use a medium weight natural yarn. Polyester won't handle as smoothly for you." Dayl couldn't remember what kind of yarn he'd picked out. He did it by color, and cost. And, as he was thinking back on it, feel. "Cast on. This time let's use a long tail." And her hands on camera were slowly casting on to the single needle. Dayl could hit pause and back up when he wanted. So this is 'remote learning' he thought. Not so bad. The Sargent continued, "Let's start with 30 stitches for practice." Dayl mimicked the Sargent and was getting the hang of casting on by number thirty. Somewhere along in there Dayl noticed the word 'Steady' had joined 'Ready' on the screen.

Having finished casting, now Sgt. Knitman instructed the viewer on how to tension the new yarn with fingers and how to roll the first stitch onto the casting needle using the second needle in the 'other' hand. Dayl saw how the second needle worked with the cast needle as Sarge began to roll down the row of cast on knots. Dayl was still slowly following along. The good Sargent continued as they worked together down the castings. And then, whoa!, turned the corner and started back. Dayl was knitting, after a fashion. And he realized that the screen was now showing 'Ready? Steady. Knit!

Somewhere amongst all the new information the Colonel-Sargent explained her knitting in the Army, Lord Kitchener and the foot soldier's socks, teaching everything from raw recruits to command staff about the Army's hows and whys, and tied them all together nicely. As a Korean War draftee who served three years all the way back in the 1950s, before computers he would add – it made sense to Dayl.

Sgt. Knitman said, "Over the years I have had the privilege to tell a lot of men where to go. And how to get there. And now I have taught you to knit." She paused for effect. "You're welcome. Dis, missed." Dayl heard himself let a little laugh escape out loud.

Video paused, Dayl intoned the Sargent's instruction. Ready? Steady. Knit! And Dayl was off and knitting. And he really didn't think about how big the fraternity he had just now joined was.

He was not quite totally absorbed when Tressa arrived home, carrying pizza. "Great minds really do think alike," he thought. And quickly stowed his 'project' and shut off the computer; he didn't want to be caught looking at how-to-knit videos by his granddaughter.

HAROLD

Chapter Eleven

H arold knew he was too late to leave the post office boxes for Dayl Carruthers, so he just kept going.

He was trying to remember where between the now closed shop and his house he could find some carry-out food to take home for Sabrina and Elsbeth. He hadn't thought of Thai food, but when the Thai Palace loomed up in front of him he made a sharp turn into the driveway.

A large sign at the entryway advised diners that the food service was curbside only. The special of the day was Garlic Chicken and Vegan Spring Rolls, or diners could request a menu to be brought to their vehicle. Believing that the special of the day was a popular meal, Harold called in an order.

Settling against the seat to wait for the take-out, Harold turned on his hand-held. He intended to monitor his favorite 2-meter repeater. The repeater was on top of a mobile phone company tower, and transmission quality was usually good.

"This is . . . WBØHVTB, traffic normal on the interstate, this is . . . K8DPOJ, debris on the roadway on Broadway, this is . . ."

Just to check in, Harold was tempted to call in from the parking lot. "Heavy dinner traffic in the Thai Palace parking lot . . ."

His finger on push-to-talk, he heard an excited transmission from KCØKLYT. "Raccoon on the Strawn OverPass, really messing up traffic. If you have an alternate route, I'd suggest you take it."

"Which end of the Strawn OverPass?"

"South end. Damn thing can't decide which way to run, just keeps working its way back and forth closer to the center."

"I feel sorry for the driver who hits it. Bust a light out or something."

"It's pretty quick-footed."

"Has anyone called animal control?"

"Looks like it. I see some red lights coming."

Absorbed in the drama of the raccoon, Harold was surprised when a Thai Palace waiter appeared at the van door. Somewhat embarrassed at not having enough cash, Harold offered a credit card. He assumed the waiter would have to go back inside for a credit card transaction, and was intrigued when the waiter took a device the size of a mobile phone from his apron pocket. He clicked a couple of buttons, scanned the card and held out the device for Harold's signature.

Back on the boulevard, Harold turned his transceiver on – maybe he would learn the fate of the raccoon.

"WA5WDKM, NN3JNJC, are you on frequency?"

"This is NN3JNJC. I'm here. What's up?"

"I just had a phone call from W8TN's daughter."

"He's a silent key."

"Yes, I remember. Great guy. He was a ham for over sixty years. His daughter has all his equipment. She says he wanted his equipment to go to handihams but she doesn't know who to contact."

"We've got at least two in the Overlake club that qualify. AA2SGFO is blind. And K3RLBC."

"K3RLBC isn't blind, but he qualifies. He's got MS . . . one of those muscular diseases."

"Did the daughter give you any kind of inventory?"

"Not yet. She said she would."

"I could contact AA2SGFO. I don't live too far from him."

"Roger on that. I'll check with K3RLBC. He's often on the air in the morning when I'm driving to work. He used to be a police dispatcher before that danged MS took him down. I'm about destinated. This is WA5WDKM signing off. 73."

"NN3JNJC. I'll be clear."

Almost home, Harold switched to his mobile phone. "Sabrina? How are you feeling? I never got those boxes to Dayl at the shop."

"That's okay. The orders can go out tomorrow."

"I'm bringing food. I'll put yours and Elsbeth's at the top of the basement stairs. I hope you like Thai food. Smells great." And thought 'darn, I shouldn't have said that'.

"I'm not hungry for much of anything. Nathan needs a change of clothes – can you take a suitcase for him over to Nana's? There's a suitcase of clothes for you. They've both been sitting on the front porch in the sunshine."

"You want me to stay at Nana's?"

"No. I want you right here in the basement. But you'll be needing a change of clothing, too, won't you?"

"Okay. I'll do it as soon as I leave your food. Can I leave it on the porch when I pick up the suitcase?"

"Yes. I'll be watching."

Sabrina was at the door, mouthing "I Love You" through the glass as Harold left the food. "I'll be right back," he mouthed in return. Trying to eat Pad Thai while driving to his mother's house was messy. Before getting out of his van, Harold pulled his mask up over his nose. What a strange world we are living in, was his uppermost thought, when people protect themselves from their own family – or their own family from them.

Nana offered Harold a cup of coffee. When Harold said "No thanks", she rebid, "I've got decaf?"

Harold shook his head again. Nathan had not made an appearance. "Sabrina tells me you went to a funeral service. I thought most people were postponing services until later. Size of gathering mandated and such."

"This was a gathering of two, the funeral home people excluded. The son was real upset he couldn't get here before his father died, and the home wouldn't let him see his dad anyway . . . a lot of people are dying lonely deaths."

Harold frowned at his next question. "How's Nathan doing?"

"He's pretty quiet. As long as he has his computer games I don't hear much from him."

"You can't tell how school is going? I wish we could keep better track of his in-school days, but I guess the teachers are having the same kind of problems." Harold paused a moment." Does he talk much to you?"

"Well . . . yes. I don't think I understand your question."

"You probably wouldn't remember Candace Phipps. From school. She's now a psychiatrist or something at the hospital. She said some kids are having . . . mental problems with the Pandemic."

"Candace Phipps? Her mother and I were room mothers when you were kids in grade school. She was a smart little fire cracker. I wouldn't be surprised at what she said, either. Nathan did ask me about his grandfather. Seems to remember more about Hank Sr. than I would have expected. It's been four years . . ." Her voice trailed off as Nathan came into the room.

"Hi, Dad."

"Hey, Buddy. How's school going?"

"Okay." Nathan almost stepped across the room to hug his dad, and then remembered he was a teenager. Dad hugs, not cool. Instead, he opened the freezer section of the refrigerator. After a moment he closed the upper door and opened the lower door.

"You're hungry," Harold observed. "What are you looking for?"

"Ice cream."

Harold rose from his seat. "There's no ice cream in this house because your grandmother never puts it on her grocery list. Come on, we'll find some ice cream . . . how about a shake? Get your jacket." Harold moved to the door. "Nana, can we bring something back for you?"

"I don't know where you're going, but if they have an orange cream shake, bring one back for me."

In the van, Nathan was quick to start a conversation. "Dad, can raccoons be pets?"

"Pets don't live as long as humans." Harold immediately wished he hadn't opened his mouth. Pets die. Animals die. Humans die, too. Nathan had already contemplated Nana's death and Harold couldn't promise him Covid wouldn't take his grandmother. He was all but certain that the raccoon had not survived being hit.

"Raccoons don't make the best pets, but it is possible to domesticate them. I knew a guy who had trained a raccoon, and then he got an appointment to West Point, and he had a hard time finding someone who would take the raccoon," Harold laughed. "Problem was, he decided West Point wasn't for him, and when he got back home, the people who had the raccoon wouldn't give it back." A moment of quiet passed in the van as the darkened neighborhoods slid by. "Uh-h, what caused this sudden interest in raccoons?"

"It was on the television news. There was a raccoon on the Strawn OverPass. A car hit it."

That was the conclusion Harold was expecting. "It's a coincidence, you hearing about it. One of the hams was up on the OverPass and kept us informed about what was happening. Last I heard he was seeing police lights." Harold was pretty sure he didn't want to be told the end of the story, and was trying to think of what he could say to Nathan. Death, as something that naturally followed life, seemed a poor consolation.

"Animal rescue came. It was moving, blinking its eyes, when they picked it up, so it was still alive," Nathan said.

Harold let out a long breath. "Looks like Jim-Pops is still open. That sound okay to you?" Harold wheeled the van into the garish glare of the busiest parking lot in town.

"Yeah." Nathan twisted in his seat. "What will animal rescue do with the raccoon?"

Harold had eased into the crowded drive-thru lane and was studying the menu offerings. "What'll you have? Can you read the menu from there?" Searching the menu himself, Harold could find no orange cream shakes.

"Yes. A banana shake." He added, "Please."

"Okay." At the order post Harold asked for a cherry shake, a vanilla shake, and " . . . what are you having?"

"Banana."

Harold turned to Nathan. "You think Nana will take a cherry shake when she asked for an orange cream?" They had reached the pay window. "There's some change over there in the door. Are there some quarters in there?"

The shakes were handed out one by one. "You don't have to wait for me," Harold said. "I'm going to offer Nana her choice – vanilla or cherry."

Nathan didn't try to identify which was the banana shake. "What will animal rescue do with the raccoon?" he repeated.

"The raccoon?" Harold waited until he was out into the flow of traffic. "They'll try to treat the injuries and when it's healed they'll release it back in the wild." If it's healed. Harold was not optimistic.

"Where is the animal shelter?"

"Over on Washington Street. You've been there. Remember when the scouts went there for a tour? Go ahead and have your shake."

"Let Nana have three choices. She might like bananas."

"That's thoughtful of you," Harold told his son.

"Dad, did you ever get that glass panel for Mom's shop made?"

"I finished it at the shop at work. It's not glass, it's a transparent plastic."

"Can I help you put it in the shop?"

"Well, sure. I'd appreciate the help. It goes next to the cash register."

Nana did like the banana, to Nathan's surprise. Harold offered Nathan the choice of vanilla or cherry. Nathan took the cherry. He carefully watched his father, and when he saw his father take a shaker of nutmeg from Nana's cabinet and liberally add the spice to his vanilla shake, he silently reached across the kitchen table and liberally covered the top of his cherry shake.

"Atta boy," Harold told his son. "Better with vanilla though."

— § —

Sabrina was waiting for Harold at the top of the basement stairs. "Did Nathan tell you tomorrow is an in-school day?"

"No, he didn't mention that."

"Well, it is. I'm exhausted and I'm going to bed, but I will call him and remind him." She didn't need to remind herself, or Harold, that she had committed them to a sidewalk sale and the get-ready clock was relentless. Two days were already lost to Covid. But she had forced herself to order inventory – start the things that could take the longest first. And having Nana's neighbor Dayl at the shop was really helping out. But Harold could see exhaustion – and Covid – on Sabrina's face.

At the foot of the steps Harold gazed upward at his wife. "How is Elsbeth? Is she showing any symptoms?

"Some. A bit of coughing. Not much appetite. She didn't like the Thai food, so I made her some mac and cheese. She's gone to bed."

"It's been a long day for everyone. How about you? How are you feeling?"

"I talked to the doctor's nurse this afternoon. As long as my symptoms stay mild she says for me to quarantine at home. What I really need is a hug."

It was all Harold could do to force himself to keep his feet planted on the basement floor. He wrapped his hands around his arms and shook himself. "How about a virtual hug?"

Sabrina rose from the step. Imitating her husband, she shook herself. "What I really want to do is plunge right down those steps. I'll take a rain check on the real thing."

Worry disturbed his dreams. Was there going to be enough time to get everything done? Harold was worried about Sabrina. In the morning they gave each other virtual hugs again.

"I'm sorry you can't come up here for breakfast."

"I'll pick up something. Where's Elsbeth? Can she tell me good-bye?" Elsbeth appeared at the top of the steps. Harold gave his daughter a virtual hug; giggling, she mimicked her father.

"Nathan wants you to bring his bike to Nana's," Sabrina remembered.

"Okay." There was barely room to ease the bicycle into the open middle section of the van.

Harold got behind the wheel.

"This is WW7PRXW. Can I get a radio check?"

"Sounds good to me. Only got a little crackle. This is AA6Y-GLK."

"Thanks. Wind last week blew my antenna down. Just got around to rectifying things."

"Got your antenna back up?"

"No. My son is going to help me on the weekend. I'm too old to be climbing up in trees."

"Roger that. My wife won't even let me get up on the roof by myself. Maybe I'll borrow your son one of these days. What are you using?"

"A J-pole. But I'm pretty close to the repeater."

"That always helps. Have you heard what we're going to have for the club program next week?"

"It'll be W4AOML, talking about disasters." WW7PRXW chuckled. "He's the guy who always lectured against self-deploying, but when that May 22 tornado hit Joplin, he self-deployed."

"We had about ten guys go to Joplin, didn't we?"

"More than that. It took down all the towers and cell service." For the first week, ham volunteers and emergency services were just about the only reliable connections across Joplin. "They didn't all go at the same time. Some of them came home and then went back down again. Brian Tallchief was there right away. Helped the Joplin guys get one of their repeater towers up again."

"Ought to be a good program."

"Roger on that. Reminds me I need to check over my go-bag. Put in some fresh batteries. I'm sure W4AOML will talk about go-bags."

"I'm at my destination. This is WW7PRXW. Thanks for the feedback. Over and out."

"AA6YGLK. Catch you next time. I'll be clear."

Harold was pleased that Nathan was watching for him at the window. At the same time he noticed that the kitchen lights were on at the Carruthers house. He reached around the rear seat for the small bundle of post office boxes. "Nathan, would you take these over to Mr. Carruthers? You know he's running the shop for your mother while she is in quarantine?" While he was waiting for Nathan, Harold took the bicycle from the van. Then he waited some more; it was taking Nathan a long time to complete a simple errand. "Ready for school?" Harold asked when Nathan finally came out of the Carruthers house. Harold noticed that Tressa followed Nathan out the door.

Harold had to wait in line to drop Nathan off at the school. "Have a good day."

"This is AB6RRDF, monitoring.'

"KC3UIUI. We've talked before. Name here's Jake."

"Yes, we have. Are you mobile?"

"No. I'm snug in my shack. How about you?"

"I'm mobile. Just got off work. Lady at the Caribbean Deli said the candy store's going to have a sidewalk sale. You know anything about that?" Word of the sidewalk sale was surely getting around.

"I heard that, too. Been wondering why. They're an essential business, been open all along."

"Gives them a chance for street-side visibility. I'm looking forward to it. Sounds like it might be a city-wide thing. Maybe there'll be some special sale prices. My budget's a little tight right now."

"Roger on that. The Mrs. always keeps me on a tight budget. I stopped getting an allowance a couple of years ago." They shared a chuckle.

"I'm about where I need to be. 73s. I'll be clear. KC3UIUI."

"AB6RRDF. Thanks for the contact."

NATHAN

Chapter Twelve

Carrying the post office boxes to Mr. Carruthers house, Nathan had been quite aware of Tressa's car in the driveway. Which meant that she had not left for work.

She was working long hours at the hospital. After Mr. Carruthers opened the door for Nathan, he couldn't believe his good luck: Tressa was seated at the kitchen table. She even remembered his name!

"Good morning, Nathan."

"Hey." Cool, he thought. He wanted to sound older.

"Off to school today? You're on a hybrid schedule too, aren't you, part in-school and part remote learning? I'm supposed to be on remote learning too, but I haven't even touched my laptop." She lifted a cup to her lips. "I think it is still in my car."

Mr. Carruthers had taken the boxes from Nathan. "Your mother's paying a lot for these when she doesn't need to. I recycled some of the boxes from the back room. I'll get some spray paint from the hardware store this morning. I can make those old boxes look like new." At Nathan's look of bewilderment Mr. Carruthers finished with, "I'll talk to Sabrina about it today."

"Where do you go to school?" Nathan asked Tressa. He knew

it wasn't exactly a correct word, but he didn't know the difference between college and university.

"South Dakota State. My major was history, but I may be changing my mind. I may go for pre-med."

Again, Nathan was baffled. He thought Tressa the most beautiful being in the entire world, there weren't any girls at his school who looked anything like Tressa, but he had no idea what a school major was. The law enforcement officer who had conducted the scouts through a tour of the city's police department was the only major he knew.

At school, Nathan pulled his mask up from his neck as he got out of the van. He had designed his mask's art work himself; he was rather pleased with his aggressive rendering of the school's mascot, a black panther. Through the glass door panels at the side of the school's entry doors he could see Alford waiting for him. Although Alford's mask was still draped around his throat, Nathan knew it said DON'T TRED ON ME!.

Nathan wished Alford weren't such a persistent shadow, but it appeared that Alford had no other friends. At lunch time Nathan tried to get in the cafeteria line next to any of the football players. He was quite relieved that his lunch time did not coincide with Alford's.

He asked his math teacher what was the difference between a college and a university, and learned that something called 'State" was likely a university. He still didn't know what a college was. He asked his science teacher what a university major was and got into a conversation about majors and minors that only confused him further.

Art was the only class Nathan shared with Alford. As he walked into the classroom Nathan was almost blown over by a huge projection on the classroom wall. It was an ancient scene, totally unfamiliar to him.

There were a number of figures in various stages of undress against a background of arches. In the center were two or more figures in military clothing. The most prominent was reaching out his arm to touch the bare chest of one of the others.

"Magnificent, isn't it?" asked the art teacher, her strong tones filling the room.

Alford remained transfixed. Nathan slowly took his seat.

"Can you imagine," the teacher continued, "a time when there was no internet? No mobile phones? Not even television? Or radio? Almost no newspapers? How did the people learn the news? How did they learn what was important?" She waited, but none of the students had a response.

"Who's the big dude in the middle?" Alford asked.

"That's Napoleon," came a voice from behind Alford.

"It's a hospital in the time of the bubonic plague," continued the teacher, ignoring the remark. "We all know what a plague is, don't we?" She paused. "It's another word for Pandemic."

"It's a hoax," came Alford's vigorous voice. He had pulled his mask away from his nose.

"I hardly think so," the teacher said. "And the bubonic plague killed millions around the world. Millions."

"It's just a game the politicians are playing so they can get more control. Closing schools, closing bars." Alford was about to go on.

Nathan glanced sideways at Alford. What did Alford know about bars?

The teacher cut off Alford's speech. She talked on about Napoleon and the plague and the Pandemic until Nathan wondered if they might be given a test some day. He'd ask his father about Napoleon Bonaparte. The teacher began asking the students to describe some detail they had discovered in the painting. "Something different that hasn't been discussed before."

Nathan's hand flew up in the air. "How can it be a hospital? There are no beds.'

"It was a hospital of the time. The name of the painting is 'Bonaparte Visits the Plague Stricken of Jaffa'. The painter was Antoine-Jean Gros."

She continued, "People were sick and dying from something that they didn't understand. Anyone thinking Covid?"

Trying to close the loop for young minds, "People were

deathly afraid of the Plague. Everywhere there was death and dying. Bodies were stacked in the graves. People were afraid to help or even touch the sick – they knew people who touched someone with the Plague who then came down with it and died. And the Plague is particularly ugly to see. It was almost a world-wide panic of death. Napoleon used large public art to convey the message to the people that their leader – Napoleon – was strong. And that he could and would survive the plague. The painting was his personal message about his invincibility while at the same time it was about hope and compassion. He wanted to lift his country up from the darkness of the deadly disease." She took a deep breath before continuing.

"Leaders want their people to have courage and a hopeful fu-ture. That's what Napoleon wanted his artist to convey. They toured the painting around countryside for people to see. Of course, being Napoleon, he couldn't help but have the artist add a little ego into the mix."

Nathan could tell that Alford had drifted somewhere else. But when the teacher asked, "Was Napoleon famous for his ego?" Alford stood up as big and tall as he could muster, pointed to the air with the index finger of his left hand, stuffed his right hand into his shirt and announced, "Who me? Dynomite!" just as the bell rang. Where, no, how does Alford come up with this stuff thought Nathan.

Alford deliberately bumped Nathan on the way out the door. Still smiling from his turn on the boards, "Why don't you come with me to my house?"

"I can't. I'm living at my grandmother's now. My mom got the virus."

"She real sick?" Nathan could tell that the irony of the 'hoax' making his mom sick was lost on Alford.

"No, not bad. Someone else is going to the store for her. Get-ting some online orders sent."

"She's not an essential business is she?"

Nathan shrugged his shoulders. "I got my bike at my grand-mother's."

"Come to my house on Saturday. Some of my uncles will be there."

At dismissal Nathan was almost the first out of the building and was pleased to see the vending company van near the front of the line of waiting vehicles. His father was talking on his handi-talky as he climbed in.

"This is KDØRVQO. Who was talking about an accident at the hospital?"

"NN3JNJC here. I think AB6RRDF was talking about it. He was driving past just after it happened, but he didn't pick up any details."

"Did he see any fire trucks?"

"He didn't say. He thought it happened in the parking garage. What's going on over there?"

Nathan noticed his dad key the mike. "KDØRVQO for ID. They're converting the covered parking garage to patient rooms. I took out some vending machines in that area because they were in the way of the new construction. They ought to be close to finishing."

"Maybe AB6RRDF will come back on. I'm pretty sure he was mobile. I think he's going to do the Traffic Light net tonight. Whoever was injured, they wouldn't have far to go for the E.R."

"Ro-ger. I'm dropping my son off at his grandmother's. I'll be back in a little. KDØRVQO. 73."

"Hey, before you go KDØRVQO, is that your wife stirring up the sidewalk sales all over?"

Embarrassed, but outted, Harold said "I don't know about stirring up . . . "

NN6JNJC continued bending the ham net protocol, "You tell her that word is that she started a great idea. Time somebody did something. Mighty oaks from small acorns grow and all that."

Swelling with pride, and news for Sabrina, Harold said simply "I'll tell her. Gotta go. KDØRVQO. 73."

"Good luck with it. Talk to you all later. NN6JNJC."

Nathan felt great about hearing good things about his

mother. Even though he wasn't entirely clear on what they were talking about. His mind was elsewhere.

Nathan headed straight for the wooden bread box at Nana's. "May I have a peanut butter sandwich?" he asked Nana, knowing her permission was automatic. For a little bit of insurance he made two sandwiches, sprinkling the peanut butter with raisins, and putting one in a baggie and stowing it in his pocket. Squished peanut butter and raisin sandwich was the best. "I'm going to be riding my bike," he shouted into the living room where Harold and Nana were still talking. He heard a soft acknowledgment in return.

His grandmother's neighborhood was new territory. He turned wheelies in the parking lot of a small church at the corner before cycling on to a busier thoroughfare two streets away. He paused as he contemplated the heavier flow of traffic. There was a rectangular blue sign with a white H and an arrow pointing forward which Nathan interpreted as symbolizing a hospital. Turning onto the sidewalk along the boulevard he followed the arrow. Several blocks later there was another big H sign with the arrow pointing to the right, but it was obvious to Nathan that he had arrived at a large hospital complex. Was it the scene of the accident he had heard discussed in the ham chatter? If he rode around the nearby blocks, would he find Tressa's car?

Tressa's little Volkswagen was two blocks away on an exclusively residential street. There was no mistake it was Tressa's car – the windows were partially blocked by her yet unpacked belongings. He lingered a few moments, tempted to leave a message on the windshield but he had neither paper nor pencil and he had no idea what message he would leave that wasn't from a kid.

The ride back to Nana's was quicker. Nana asked Nathan if he had had a good ride and asked him to help her set the table for supper. After the dinner meal Nathan sat his laptop at a small table near a window where he had a partial view of the Carruthers driveway; he spent some time looking at maps on the internet and routing the path from Nana's to the animal shelter. Mr. Carruthers' car appeared around six pm, but there was no other car in the driveway when Nana reminded Nathan that it was his bedtime.

— § —

Tressa's car was in the driveway when Nathan woke up in the morning. He was at breakfast when he saw Tressa emerge from the Carruthers house. He jumped up from his chair and bolted for the door, but the best he could manage was a wave from the doorway. He was pleased to see that Tressa gave him a wave in return.

"Is that your father?" Nana asked. "Come to take you to school?"

"No. This is a remote day. I'm going to get started as soon as I can."

The online classes went well. After lunch Nathan decided to skip art class – he really didn't want to hear more about Napoleon at Jaffa. He told Nana he was going to ride his bike home to get something he needed from the basement.

Nathan knew that the route to the animal shelter would take him close to Alford's house. He kept telling himself he definitely was not going to detour past Alford's but at the last minute he impulsively made the turn. Alford was in the driveway tossing a tennis ball against a wooden garage door.

"Yo," Alford shouted at Nathan. "Whassup?"

"I'm going to the animal shelter. You wanna go with me?"

"Why are you going there?"

"I dunno. Look at the animals."

"How? I ain't gonna walk that far."

"I'll ride you on my bike."

"Naw. Wait a minute." Alford disappeared around the rear of the house.

Nathan waited for what he thought was more than five minutes and was considering following Alford around the rear to see if he could determine where Alford had gone when he heard a call from the street.

Alford, mounted on a bicycle, was making large circles in the street. "Are you coming or not?"

It took them a bit longer than Nathan had anticipated. At the entryway of the animal shelter there was a convenient bike rack. Nathan led the way inside, but they waited a few minutes in the lobby before anyone noticed their presence.

The air was alive with animal noises, mostly barking dogs, but Nathan thought he could hear faint meowing cries, and a strange clapping sound that could be ducks.

A tall, stocky black man carrying a rolled up hose noticed them first. "Hey, Ms. Switzer?" he called back into the interior of the building. "Your walkers are here."

Within seconds a woman with short grey hair, wearing an oversize sweat shirt with a giant pink paw print appeared with several animal leashes in her hands. "Have you boys ever done this before?"

Uncertain about how he should reply, Nathan gave a negative shake of his head. After a glance at Nathan, Alford followed his example.

The woman hardly looked at them. She untangled the leashes and gave each boy a leash to hold. "We're so short-handed . . . two of our regular walkers have the virus. Come on down this hall . . . some of our dogs didn't get walked yesterday. They'll be pretty feisty, but you look like you're strong enough to handle it." She stopped at a counter built into the wall. "Let's get you signed in . . . fill out a name tag. Sweeney's already outside and he'll help you keep track of which dogs you walk. We need to know how long too."

Bewildered, Alford looked at Nathan, who shrugged his shoulders to show his friend that he was willing to take whatever happened. Within moments they were in front of Sweeney, the tall, stocky man they had met at the entryway. Sweeney led them to a room full of animal cages. He motioned to Alford as he opened one of the cages. "This here is Torch," Sweeney said, letting a red-furred spaniel out of the cage. She didn't get walked yesterday, don't let her knock you off your feet." Sweeney motioned Nathan to follow him to another cage. "This here is a rare golden retriever. We call her Snowy, because instead of being yellow, she's pure white. She wasn't walked yesterday either." While Sweeney talked, he took the leashes from Alford and Nathan, fastened them to the dogs' collars and returned them to the boys. "Hang on to these. You'll be in a fenced-in field, so don't worry about them getting away from you, but we need to keep them on leash for control. If they get adopted, they'll still have to be accustomed to a leash." He swung Snowy's cage door shut. "Now let me show you where the walking field is." He took a large ring of keys from his belt.

Alford, with Torch, was close behind Sweeney. As the excited animal brushed against Alford's legs, Alford reached down to scratch the back of Torch's neck. Torch swung her head back to lick Alford's fingers.

Sweeney kept them busy changing out dogs. He had brought them four sets of dogs to be walked when he asked them if they were up to a real challenge. When they agreed, although a bit hesitant, he brought out to the walking area a bushel basket full of puppies. "They're only four weeks old and they're driving their mother crazy. Just let them run about ten minutes."

Nathan was surprised when Sweeney appeared again, yelling "Time's up. Come along little dawggies, come along." He started picking up puppies and putting them back in the basket. "Their mother's getting restless, wants them back." Alford and Nathan helped corral the last of the puppies.

"Mrs. Switzer wants to thank both of you and hopes you will come back to help us again."

"Where's the raccoon?" Nathan blurted. "Can we see the raccoon?"

Sweeney looked surprised. "How'd you know we have a raccoon?"

Nathan fibbed. "It was in the news."

"I'll show you on the way out. Mr. Raccoon was hurt pretty

bad in the accident – may not make it."

Sweeney led the boys through the interior of the building to a room that resembled a doctor's office. An inert raccoon lay in a dog bed on top of a cart against the far wall. All four of the animal's legs were wrapped in tape and gauze. Nathan slowly approached the raccoon.

Nathan did not notice the woman in the room until she spoke to him. "We never had a raccoon before," she said. "We don't think he's going to make it. The vet said he might. You want to touch him? Very softly. He's somewhat sedated." Nathan remembered what sedated meant.

Emboldened, Nathan put his hand on the raccoon's back and gently massaged with his fingers. The creature's eyes fluttered. Nathan leaned over to speak to the animal. "Keep fighting, Buddy." The fur felt soft and smooth under the palm of his hand.

Mrs. Switzer saw them to the lobby. She read from the information forms. "Nathan and Alford. We really appreciate your time." She handed them each a 'Friend to the Animals' card with their names filled in to keep in their billfolds. Which Nathan didn't have but realized he would need to get if he was going to be a real grownup. Mrs. Switzer asked, "Will you be able to help us again?"

"Not tomorrow, but the next day," Nathan promised. He looked at Alford, hoping for his agreement, but either way, Nathan planned to be at the shelter again. Tomorrow, he remembered, would be an in-school day. As he took his bicycle from the rack his mobile phone vibrated and he realized that Nana had tried to call him two times before. "Nana? I'm heading home."

"Where are you? Why didn't you answer before?"

"I'm with Alford. I'm coming right home."

Both boys mounted their bicycles with haste and began peddling furiously. Nathan did not try to follow Alford to his house, but kept on the quickest route. Shortly after separating from Alford, Nathan felt his mobile phone vibrate again.

"Nathan? I thought you were coming home. Where are you?"

"I'm coming. I'll explain when I get there." Nathan had already convinced himself that Nana would be satisfied with nothing but the truth.

Tressa turned into the Carruthers driveway just before Nathan reached Nana's driveway. As Tressa emerged from her car she noticed Nathan, gave him a wave and appeared to be willing to stop for a chat. Nathan returned the wave and kept moving. As encouraged as he might be at any sign of friendliness, it was more important to keep Nana happy.

Nathan was beginning to understand the grownup world: Happy Nana, happy life. What he teenaged oblivious too, for the moment, was how many of the grownups around him were focused, each on their own converging timeline, on helping Sabrina through Covid and on to a successful sidewalk sale to buoy the yarn shop. There was a little over a week to go to the sidewalk sale. A lot can happen in a week.

TRESSA

Chapter Thirteen

T ressa was puzzled at Nathan's abrupt behavior. Previously he seemed eager to talk with her.

She watched as he left his bicycle on the back side of the house and ran in through the side door. Kids. Maybe she had misinterpreted his actions in her presence.

She deliberately made extra noise as she came into the Carruthers house and took her time moving from the kitchen into the living room. Even so, she was in sight of her grandfather in time to see him push something colorful behind the chairside magazine rack at the side of his recliner. Besides trying to keep some project hidden from her eyes, she had caught him nervously turning off his laptop to keep her from seeing what he was watching.

She stilled a laugh; her Grandmother Emmie would have enjoyed Grandpa Dayl's anxiety – Grandpa Dayl was watching YouTube in an effort to teach himself how to knit. Grandmother Emmie was a quilter, but she also knew how to knit and would have been delighted at his interest in learning. She herself could probably have remembered well enough to teach him the basics. She missed her. They missed her.

With Grandpa helping out at Mrs. Harkins' daughter-in-law's knit shop, maybe she'd start a project for herself. If she wasn't working such long hours at the hospital.

She was a screener. She had two re-purposed green auxiliary jackets and the Human Resources department had made her a very official appearing name tag. The tag said she was a 'patient adviser' but in truth she was a screener. She took the temperatures of any visitor who came in through the front lobby and consulted the patient list which designated whether the patient was permitted to have visitors. Only one visitor at a time and only two total per day. Zero visitors in the Covid wards. It was heart-breaking when Tressa had to turn someone away. Hospital security was always somewhere in the lobby to help if needed. Doubly sad.

His hand still poking something under the magazine rack, Dayl remarked to Tressa, "You're home early. I haven't made any plans for supper."

"You haven't hidden the can opener, have you? I still know how to open a can. Let me go see what I can find in the cupboard," she said, but she sat down in the chair across from her grandfather instead. "How's the yarn shop business?"

"I'm learning a lot. It's more complicated that you might think. And Sabrina wants us to get ready to hold a big sidewalk sale at the end of next week. That's, like, tomorrow," said Dayl sounding more like a college kid than he realized. Tressa thought that she could see her grandfather making a mental to-get-done list. With him busy working, she was seeing him in a new light – not just Grandpa, but an adult. Like her.

"I used to know how to knit. Maybe I'll start another project while I'm here." She wheedled, "Uh-h-h, have you been talking recently to your friend, Mr. Garretson?"

"Vince? No. Why do you ask?"

"His son, Jay, is in the hospital. Came in through the E.R. late this afternoon. He was admitted as a patient. I'm not supposed to know but I think it is Covid."

Dayl looked at his watch. "Sorry to hear that. Maybe I'll call

Vince after supper."

Tressa jumped up. "Supper? What are we going to have for supper?" The kitchen and pantry had always been well-organized when her Grandmother Emmie was still alive. Under Grandpa's management – or lack of – it was hard to find anything. And things were running more quickly amok with Grandpa working at the knit shop, absently carrying around bamboo knitting needles; there certainly was more to Grandpa than Tressa ever knew.

Tressa looked first in the freezer top of the refrigerator. Everything she found had long since passed an expiration date. She made herself a note to ask Grandpa for the best way to discard the overdue food. In the pantry she found a can of chili meat, and many cans of different beans: kidney beans, dark and light navy beans, barbecue beans, black beans, cannelloni beans, even garbanzo beans. He must run on beans, she thought, smiling. She set the chili-meat can and the navy beans and black beans on the counter and began a search for a can opener. She wasn't quite ready, yet, to look into how Grandpa was keeping Emmie's spice cabinet. The chili wouldn't be as hot as her friends liked it. But that might be for the better she thought.

Her mind tracked back to earlier in the afternoon when with a jolt, Jeremiah Garretson's name had popped up on the patient admit list. It was Jay. The boy, young man, she met that first day with Grandpa.

In her first days at the hospital she had shadowed one of the RN's, and had a general idea of the locations of the different departments. Jay had come in through the E.R., and had been transferred to an ICU on the third floor. She was pretty sure it was the Covid triage ward. Her job as a screener kept her limited to the first floor lobby. She couldn't – at the moment – think of any reason she could possibly invent that would give her reason for going to the third floor.

The simplified patient list available to her on the screener's computer terminal gave no information about the reason that had brought a patient to the hospital, although some wards, like the cardiac ward and the birthing center, obviously were for patients with specific needs. The Pandemic, however, had created confusion.

Tressa found no can opener on any of the counter spaces; she began opening drawers.

In her mind she could see the hospital parking building where Vince Garretson had given the unicycle to Jay. In turn, Jay had immediately tried to ride the unicycle, taking a spectacular tumble onto the concrete. She had no doubt that off the job Jay had continued his attempts to master the unicycle; to push her dread of Covid aside, she could easily imagine another mishap serious enough to land him in the E.R. What possible errand could she create that would take her to the third floor? Her young mind found it hard to even imagine being that alone and frightened in a sea of masked strangers. Closing the last drawer, she went to the kitchen doorway. "Grandpa, I can't find that can opener Anna gave you."

"There are several in the top left-hand drawer, next to the sink," answered Dayl.

Tressa could hear sounds of movements.

"I'll be right there." Dayl opened a drawer Tressa had looked in previously. He laid two pieces of equipment on the counter. "Either one of these will work." He removed another tool, a wicked looking piece of metal with a miniature bayonet at the end. With his fingers he took out a smaller, hinged object. "Here's the GI can opener. Anna's joke on me." His hand went back to a white plastic opener with a couple of buttons, or small levers, that were red in color. "This one works for me."

Tressa knew now that her widower grandfather had intentionally lied to the widow next door about his lack of domestic wherewithal. "Don't you have an electric opener?"

"Emmie never wanted one." Dayl reached for one of the cans, swapping the navy beans for one of dark red kidney beans.. "Is this what you need open?"

"Well, you're going to have an electric opener now." She remembered passing a kitchen gadget store. They might be open as an essential business; if not, they might be reachable through a website.

Dayl lifted the round metal lid from the can of chili meat. She took the opener from his hands and tried without success to attach the small bladed wheel on the rim. Dayl reclaimed the opener, fitted it onto the next can and stepped back to let Tressa turn the knob. Darned good chili out of a can.

With Tressa's added special secret ingredient, a dusting of pumpkin pie spice, the chili was on the table in short order.

Tressa decided she should learn more from Anna.

She remembered something Grandma Emmie used to say: 'The difference between knowing and learning is doing.' Emmie and Anna, almost the same age and the same kind of strong women who knew and did so much. She wondered, and then thought better: she had enough on her plate without trying to play matchmaker for her grandfather.

While Dayl was still finishing supper, Tressa began loading the dishwasher. Dayl's plate was the last item to be slipped into a slot; Tressa asked him to start the dishwasher as she watched. When they were both back in the living room, she reminded Dayl about calling his friend, Vince Garretson. At no answer, he left a recorded message.

Frustrated, Tressa asked Dayl about the Garretson family. "How long have you known them?"

"Oh, twenty, maybe thirty years. We're not that well acquainted. We're lodge brothers. Except I don't go to the lodge much any more."

"How many children did Mr. Garretson have?"

"A couple. Maybe three. He's a fair bit younger than I am. Your father might have known him in high school."

"He's got at least one son, that Jay, who we saw when you took him the unicycle."

Dayl laughed. "We were quite a show, at least twenty of us, parading around with those unicycles. Emmie never wanted me to do it."

"I can understand that. They look quite dangerous to me."

"There's a knack to it. I didn't want you to think you could ride one – although you probably could."

"I've got to do a laundry so I will have clean scrubs tomorrow. Anything you want to toss in?"

"Not this time."

As far as Tressa knew, Jay's father did not return the call.

Across the breakfast table she watched her grandfather shake cereal into a big bowl along with more whole milk than she thought someone his age should be having. She took the box away from him to read the ingredients. "You know," she told him, "this 'good stuff' is bad for you."

"Emmie used to cook oats . . . or cracked wheat."

"You could learn to cook oats . . . or wheat."

"She let me put brown sugar on it."

"Brown sugar is okay."

" . . . and raisins . . . "

"I use stevia when I can get it."

"Stevia who?" Dayl reached for a small notepad. "You get that at the grocery store? I can put it on the list."

Tressa pulled the notepad away from Dayl. She wrote the word 'stevia', followed by 'greenleaf'. "It's a natural product. It's not an artificial sweetener."

"Maybe the grocery store people can help me find it."

"Maybe I can go shopping with you." She was busy adding yogurt to the list, and crossing off ice cream. She had no idea why he had written chocolate mint cookies on their list and she didn't know that he knew what biscotti were. Or what they were for.

Tressa delayed her departure as long as she could, but there was no return call from Mr. Garretson that morning. She was lucky to find a parking place a bit closer to the hospital than usual. She was at her place inside the main lobby five minutes ahead of schedule. Her work station seemed to face a never ending stream of people who needed scanning for fever, directions, assistance, instructions, a face to talk to.

Although there was something familiar about the first person through the door, she couldn't place him. A middle-aged, stocky man in work clothing, hard hat hanging from his belt. She readied the thermometer to scan his forehead.

"No, you don't need to do that, I was checked at the employee entrance. I work here. I'm not coming to see anyone. My son's a patient here and I brought him something."

"Do you know your son's room number? What's his name?." She had her fingers poised over the computer which was on a high stool near the doorway. She still hadn't connected the dots.

"I don't know if he has a room yet. He was in ICU. His name is Jeremiah Garretson."

Tressa's fingers froze in position over the keyboard. Vince Garretson needed someone to deliver something to his son, Jay? What Tressa had been plotting, and scheming and pondering had fallen right into her hands. "Is this urgent? Is he expecting it right away?" If it were urgent, she could find someone to make a quick trip to the third floor. If not, if it could wait until her morning break ... Tressa's head was spinning.

"I wouldn't say its urgent ... but he is expecting it." He held out a plastic sack. "Aren't you Dayl Carruthers granddaughter? Didn't I meet you the other day when your grandfather brought me his unicycle?"

"Yes, yes you did. You encouraged me to check in with HR. And it all happened so fast and here I am and this has all been so very interesting and so ... ." Tressa realized she was saying too much, too fast, so she finished, ... "educational." And then added, "Thank you."

Vince said, "Well, Daylor's granddaughter, I am sure we are lucky to find you so don't thank me, thank you. And good luck."

Tressa heard herself blurt out: "Does Jay have the virus?"

"I don't know if it's good news or bad, but he doesn't have Covid. He was in a boom truck when something failed. He went down like an elevator. I saw it happen, right back there in the parking garage. Broke a couple of bones. Well, mostly cracked luckily enough. But a concussion. Docs think he's going to recover nicely, but it will take some time. He'll be here a couple of days to monitor."

"I'm sorry to hear that. I'm so glad for him. I mean glad it isn't Covid. You can be sure Jay will get these things. I will make certain of that personally." A pause. "Right away," she said.

Vince gave her a wink as he left which made Tressa wonder if he could possibly be reading her mind. Tressa waited in vain for someone to come give her a morning break. No one came until almost noon when Grace Tilley, showed up, sack lunch in hand. "Hi, Tressa. Thought I'd come down to see if you needed a break."

"Sure could."

"I brought my lunch. I'll eat here at your desk while you get something for yourself. Give you a little break. I think I can handle the thermometer for a while. The CEO sent word down that we really appreciate your work."

"Well, you're welcome, but all of this is so interesting and so helpful..."

Nurse Tilley continued. "You just pitched right in and got right to work. You're the kind of person health care needs. You have made yourself quite useful. Sorry there wasn't much training."

"It's been good for me. There's been enough training to get started."

"Well, you've been so helpful," said Grace, "we're glad you made time to join us."

In the elevator up to the third floor Tressa couldn't resist a look into the plastic bag. She found a notebook, a packet of ink pens, a wrist watch, a razor, and stamped envelopes. She stepped out onto the third floor. Nurses, aides, and other hospital employees, even a security guard moved up and down the hallways, but the nursing station was empty. Which room was Jay's? Two nurses stopped near Tressa but neither one turned to ask how they could help her; they engaged in their own conversations.

"Room 311 goes to surgery next. About fifteen minutes." The woman motioned down the east-bound hall."

"I can help you with that. Garretson goes in thirty minutes," the other woman said. "Someone should tell Vince. I saw him in the building earlier."

"Where is the patient?" She moved down the hall. "You know his father is in charge of maintenance."

"Room 323." Following the first nurse, the second motioned down the south-bound hall.

Neither one looked at Tressa. Slowly, Tressa walked down the hallway, checking room numbers as she went. The door to Room 323 was ajar. Without hesitation, she walked in. One of the two beds was unoccupied at the moment; the other held the inert body of a young man, connected with tubes and wires. Jay Garretson. Jay's eyes were closed, his chest moving slightly. Tressa guessed he was probably asleep; if he were in a coma he would still be in an ICU bed. She didn't want to wake him, but if he was scheduled for surgery, he would soon be awakened.

"Jay?" she said tentatively.

There was no response.

"Jay?"

The breathing remained regular, uninterrupted. Easy. Tressa liked the sound.

"Jay, your father brought some things to the hospital for you." She opened the plastic bag. "A notebook, Some ink pens. Envelopes with stamps. A wrist watch –"

"Put it on." The words were low and weak. Jay's left arm moved closer to the edge of the bed.

"The wrist watch?" Tressa was beyond startled.

"Yes." The reply was a hoarse whisper.

The watch band was thick, heavy leather with signs of usage. Tressa opened the buckle and reached for Jay's hand. Gently, she positioned the watch around Jay's wrist and slid the buckle prong into the most used hole in the leather band. As she slid her hand away she was astonished to feel his fingers tighten into a grip. She did not resist, but she wondered if it were an involuntary response. She studied the watch, clearly an older model. She studied his face, clearly a newer model, she thought; and that made her smile.

One of the nurses from the hallway – Naydene on her name tag – came hastily into the room and checked the various monitors. "We'll be taking you to surgery in a few minutes," she announced to the room. She appeared to be watching for any facial movement; Jay's eyes remained closed without response.

"I have to go now." Tressa leaned over to speak softly in Jay's ear, but as she tried to disentangle her fingers she felt the renewed pressure of a tightened grip.

The nurse moved to the door. "I'll be right back," Naydene promised.

Right back stretched into several minutes; Jay's grip relaxed. Only a bit.

Naydene was accompanied by another nurse when she returned. They both began disconnecting, or sometimes reconnecting, the drip lines and monitors. Smooth, efficient, practiced, professional, thought Tressa. She spoke softly again at Jay's ear. "It's time for your surgery," but at the slightest move of her fingers, the grip tightened again. She looked at Naydene. "His father brought a wrist watch to the hospital and . . . Jay . . . wanted me to put it on."

With a glance Naydene confirmed for herself what Tressa had told her. "He can't wear that in the operating room anyway." She was easily at Tressa's side, removing the watch. Jay's grip on Tressa's hand did not ease. "We can put it with his belongings, there in the drawer, or you can keep it for him until he comes out of anesthesia." She put the watch in Tressa's free hand. The other nurse was already rolling the head of Jay's bed away from the wall. She gave Tressa a nod which Tressa interpreted as permission to continue to hold Jay's hand. They moved out into the hall and onto the elevator which fortunately was large enough for a hospital bed and its makeshift entourage. At the second floor they were soon at double swinging doors marked NO ADMITTANCE.

"You really are going to have to let your friend go," Naydene said to Jay, her tone gentle. "She'll keep your watch for you."

Jay's fingers tightened. Jay surprised all of them by asking, "What's your name?"

"Tressa Carruthers." She felt his hand loosen. She lifted his arm to lay it alongside his body and gave his hand one last squeeze. After he was gone she remained a few moments staring at the NO ADMITTANCE letters. Naydene, coming back out of the operating room area, jolted Tressa back into movement. "You don't have to go home, but you can't stay here." Tressa made her way slowly back to the main lobby.

"How was lunch?" Grace Tilley asked but before Tressa could tell her she'd skipped lunch a doctor strode in and drew Grace away. "Excuse me," Grace said back over her shoulder. And was gone.

The afternoon went by like a dream. A very fast dream. Tressa was scheduled to work a twelve-hour day, with two meal breaks. Not having had lunch, Tressa chose a peanut bar and a soft drink from the vending machines in a nearby nook. At the second break she headed straight for the third floor.

The occupant of Room 323 was sound asleep. Tressa found Naydene at the nursing station. "Room 323? Jay Garretson. He came through fine, and now he's sleeping. Sedated. He had some serious injuries, mostly the right leg, but he'll recover quickly."

Tressa held up her hand. "I still have his watch. Could I return it to him?" Naydene, her eyes on the computer screen in front of her, gave a permissive nod. Tressa walked down the darkened hallway and back into room 323. Jay was obviously in the land of slumber as well as the occupant of the other bed.

With a light touch, she put the wrist watch on Jay's left arm. She opened the packet of ink pens Jay's father had sent and tore a page out of the notebook.

Hi, Jay. I put your watch on your wrist. The nurse says you came through the surgery fine. I will try to visit you tomorrow. Tressa Carruthers.

The pen paused while she thought about adding her phone

number. She made a heart by her name instead.

HAROLD

Chapter Fourteen

Harold kept waiting for Nathan to ask him the question. It was inevitable. Kids and pets. Both Nathan and Alford had become regular walkers at the animal shelter.

Nana had been quick to gather details from Nathan. Once discovered, a transportation plan was put in place. A little preteenage responsibility and compassion for others was a good idea. On remote learning days Nathan and Alford rode bicycles to the shelter. Harold picked them up; the bicycles were hauled in the van.

Alford was voluble about the dog he wanted to adopt. At first it was any dog; later he was specific, although frequently changing his mind. Sometimes his chosen dog was adopted by another family. Alford's problem was getting approval from a parent, plus the adoption fees, but Harold suspected the shelter could waive the fees if Alford could get permission. Nathan, strangely, remained silent about the question they all were expecting with his sudden interest in the shelter.

Up and down the basement staircase Harold and Sabrina had discussed the possibility of having a dog come to live at the Harkins' house, after Elsbeth had gone to bed. It was hard to really talk things over when they were separated by the basement steps. Sabrina sat on the kitchen floor, her legs stretched down in front of her. Harold began with sitting on the second step from the bottom, but he tired of twisting to face her and found a three-legged stool he could use while propping against the cold concrete blocks. Sabrina began to think of these nightly conversations as their Romeo-and-Juliet moments.

"Nathan finally asked me," Sabrina revealed.

"About getting a dog instead of having a birthday party?"

"He promised that if we would let him get a pet he would be very responsible about taking care of it."

"Does he know that there are some charges, some fees, in connection with adopting a dog?" Harold asked.

"He's kind of vague, but I think he knows."

"What about Elsbeth? Will she want a kitten for her birthday? I can't see us having a cat, and a dog."

Sabrina groaned. "Me neither. But she understands that with the virus none of her friends are having birthday parties. She only wants me to knit her some pink baby bunnies to go with the floppy-eared mama rabbit she already has."

Harold sighed. "Well, that seems simple enough."

"Easy for you to say – they're small, but she wants six – one for each year."

Harold joined her in a groan, he knew better than to chuckle. "I can't help you with that."

"Oh, I can do it – just takes a lot of time."

They let a calming, quiet moment pass between them. Bliss.

"We could call it the family dog," Harold suggested, hopefully.

"There's some kind of procedure, isn't there? Nathan won't just show up some day with a dog?"

"No. That's what's holding Alford up. If he could get someone in his family to agree, he'd have a big dog yesterday."

"That might mature Alford a little. How much does it cost?"

"There are some fees. And you have to get a city license."

"Alford's family doesn't have that kind of money. Even after you get them, pets are expensive."

"I know." His wife looked so downhearted Harold wanted to bound up the steps and give her a hug.

"How big a dog do you think Nathan wants?"

"I can't tell. He talks about them by names. They all have name tags and the shelter people encourage the walkers to use the animal's name." Harold caught a glimpse of Elsbeth, clad in her sleepers, silently padding up behind Sabrina. Harold asked, "How are things going at the shop? Anything I can help you with? Do you think Dayl has a handle on it?"

Sabrina was startled as Elsbeth put her arms around Sabrina's neck from the rear. "Oh, sweetie, what are you doing awake?"

"I want Daddy to put me to bed."

Harold's voice was soft. "Not until you get over the Covid, sweetie. You be a good girl for Mommy and when your fever is gone I'll take you both to the ice cream shop. Any flavor you want. Triple dip. Maybe some coconut and a cherry on top."

Elsbeth smiled a sick child smile.

"I'll read you a story," Sabrina offered as she hugged the sweeter other half of her Covid bubble. "There is something you can drop off at the shop tomorrow," she told Harold. "We're having pretty good sales of Chameleon Scarf kits. I've re-written the instructions. Dayl can make extra copies on the printer."

Harold's phone woke him in the morning, never a good sign. Especially when caller ID indicated the call was coming from his boss, Arney Faulkner. "Harkins here," he said, and was alarmed to hear sounds of crying.

"This is Irene Faulkner," came between the sobs "Arney is in the hospital. The virus. He couldn't breathe last night."

"Sorry to hear that."

"They put him in a ventilator right away."

"I talked to him yesterday. He didn't say a thing about not feeling well."

"He never does. Always believes he'll get better." The sobs overcame her again.

"How can I help?"

"I'm going over to the office to get the phone calls. But I have some papers he will need at the hospital. Can you take them? You can get in with all of our work over there."

"Sure. Where will you be? At the office or at the house?"

"At the office. I'll be there by eight."

"I'll be there a little after eight." He tried to think of something reassuring to say. "Arney will be okay. There are a lot of good people at the hospital."

"I hope so." Irene Faulkner was still crying when she hung up the phone.

Harold called up the basement steps. "Do you have a get-well card on hand?"

Sabrina came to the door, opened it wide. "Who for?"

"My boss. Mrs. Faulkner called. Says Arney's on a ventilator."

"Oh, dear, that's bad news."

Harold was moving fast when he reached Nana's. He wouldn't even have time to have coffee. Or come inside. He called ahead instead. Nathan was on the steps when Harold pulled in. At this point in his life Harold was not prepared to buy into a business, even a business he knew like the back of his hand. And if he couldn't afford to invest in the vending machine business, would he even have a job? "You won't be at the shelter today, will you?" At Nathan's headshake, Harold felt relieved; the matter of a dog was likely to be moved one more day down the road; maybe if this &#*%$#&^*& Pandemic were over with they could start living a normal life again; except the old normal was never coming back; life would be a new normal. If Arney Faulkner died of Covid-19, what would happen to the vending machine business? Harold was deep in thought.

"Dad, what's a dummy load?"

"A dummy load?" Harold started as if he had never heard of such a thing before. He closed his mouth. Nathan's question meant, somehow, that he had been looking at the technician license study manual. "A dummy load," Harold began more slowly. "It's a device you use for testing purposes. Radio testing. Ham radio. I can show you when we are back at the house."

"Okay."

Irene Faulkner's eyes were still red. She had worked part-time, off and on, in the business keeping the books, invoicing, even collecting from time to time, so she wasn't a total stranger to what needed to be done. She handed Harold a small manila envelope. "They told me I could leave the papers, but I wouldn't be permitted to see Arnold. I thought we'd be better off with me here to take the phone calls."

"That's probably true, but you know, with so many offices closed, people working at home, there's not the demand for vending machines as before." Harold refrained from voicing his opinion that the vending business might not ever recover its pre-Pandemic levels. Now was not the time. He also withheld asking what she would do about the business if Arney did not survive. Now was really not the time. Too soon, much too soon. Too uncertain. Everybody needed to work through Covid first. Besides, he knew that he was married to a glass-half-full optimist planning a sidewalk sale to save her business from what could be her deathbed. So far, Harold had not caught her Covid, maybe he should catch her optimism.

"K8DPOJ monitoring. Is anybody on frequency?"

"WW7PRXW back at you. What's going on in your world?"

"Raining out here on the western fringes. What's it doing where you are?"

"It's clouding up, Pete. Looks like you're sending it our way. WW7PRXW for ID."

"I'll call the weatherman and see what I can do about that."

"Call Stan. He's the one with the inside track with the weatherman."

"We've got a couple of new hams this week. One of them got a new HT at the candy store, but the other one is kind of lost with not much money. Do we have anything in the lending library?"

"This is KD0RVQO, Harold. I've got an extra HT I can let go of for a while."

"W8TN's daughter is looking for a home for his equipment. You know he's a silent key. Do you think she'd consider a new ham a worthy recipient?"

148

"I don't know, but she might give some of it to the club, and we could lend it out."

"Some of that stuff W8TN had were boat anchors. He was the only guy who could make that gear go! KC3UIUI for ID."

"Boat anchors? That's my cup of tea. Who has boat anchors? This is AB6RRDF."

"W8TN's daughter. She'd probably be satisfied to see them go to a happy home."

"I'll get in touch with her. Let you get back to your rag-chew. AB6RRDF. 73."

"Who had an HT they could part with short term?"

"I did. KD0RVQO. I'm pulling into my parking lot."

"Can I pick that up from you tonight? I'll get it to the new guy. And since he isn't spending money for a rig, he can afford to join the club."

"Club membership is free the first year," said Stan, "KØLLHA."

Harold turned off his handi-talky. He parked the van next to some of the hospital maintenance vehicles and entered through the E.R.

Harold thought Arney would be on the fourth floor south. Harold knew exactly where that was. He was wearing his Overlake Vending Machine Company jacket, which confused the nurse at the fourth floor south nurse's station. "You're not here to work on the vending machines?"

"No," he went with honesty as the best policy, "I've brought some papers for a patient, my boss, Arnold Faulkner."

The nurse checked the roster. "He's not here. He's in . . ." She studied the computer screen. "He's on the ground floor . . . that's the converted garage. You know how to get there?"

"Sure do."

"You know you're bending the rules, right?"

"Sure do," he repeated. "Thanks." Harold was interested in the opportunity to view the working insides of the converted space he had just been in while still a garage. A nurses' station was immediately inside the door. From what Harold could see, the space was now divided by canvas walls into patient rooms separated by a hallway that made a square-cornered interior loop. The dominant color was a white so pure it was almost blinding. The light panels in the hallway ceiling amplified the effect. Kitchen staff was busy clearing away the dirty dishes from a breakfast meal. In a small offset space was a break room, where Harold had installed the new vending machines.

Of course, Harold knew where every vending machine in the hospital was located, but he had no idea where Candace Phipps had her office. Delivering the manila envelope for his boss to the nursing station, Harold asked where he would find Candace's office. On the fifth floor, he was told, outside of the Covid barrier.

Harold went to find her. He saw Candace in the fifth floor hallway, and followed her to her office. "I think I am lucky to have run into you. Have you got a few spare minutes?"

"Of course." She motioned him inside, offered him a chair. She was wearing a mask adorned with tumbling bunnies.

"What did you tell me the other day about how children are dealing with the Pandemic?"

"Some of them are not doing too well. I'm sure they are reflecting the anxieties of their parents and the adults around them. You have two kids, don't you?"

"Yes. It's my son I'm worried about. He's twelve. He's been walking dogs at the animal shelter and now he wants to adopt a dog."

"That's not surprising."

"Our lives are so unstable now. I might not have a job next year – my boss is here right now on a ventilator. Sabrina is worried about having to close the yarn shop. She's quarantined at home with Elsbeth. No bad symptoms so far for either of them but Sabrina seems to be wearing down."

"Even if you try to keep this from your children, they are absorbing some of your anxiety. You and your wife need to act as calm as you possibly can. Are there any other adults your children are close to?"

"Their grandmother, Nana. She's been taking care of them

while the schedules are so crazy. Nathan is living at her house now." Harold stopped while he pondered Nana's reaction to Nathan having a dog. "Sabrina and Elsbeth are in quarantining at home. They've both got the virus. I think I said that. Thankfully so far, pretty mild. I'm sleeping in the basement, sharing with the furnace and the appliances . . . "

"Right there . . . there are a lot of deviations from normal. How old is Elsbeth?"

"She's almost six."

"Some of the responses we are seeing are from very young children. Do either of them have nightmares?"

"Not that I am aware of. They're more likely to tell their mother if they do."

"Are they eating regularly? Sometimes that is a tell-tale sign."

"Nathan eats like a horse." Harold was trying to think back.

"Not surprising at his age. But long story short, children learn about responsibility by taking care of an animal."

Harold realized he was taking up her time in an unscheduled visit, but there was one more urgent matter – the most urgent matter – that he wanted to talk to Candace about. He found it hard to talk about the matter himself.

"Nathan's grandfather – my father – died about four years ago, but the other day Nathan asked me when his grandmother was going to die. Like he thought it might happen any minute."

"I remember your mother. She was a room mother the same year as my mother. Has she been ill?"

"No, thank heavens. She's a rock. But a small one," he quickly added. "We had been waiting for her to give up the house and move into a care facility. Luckily, that didn't happen. It would have turned out to be a disaster, what the Pandemic is doing to nursing homes."

Candace rolled her eyes in agreement. "So she's still in her house? Keeping herself isolated, I hope. Do you know if she has given Nathan any clues about not feeling well?"

"I doubt it. She's not one to complain."

"Well, it's a tough call. And it's things like this that are causing some concerns with some of our children, especially if they have already lost a relative or another person in their life. You could reassure Nathan that his grandmother is still going to be with the family in the foreseeable future, and then she could become ill, or some other unexpected event, and Nathan would lose trust in you."

They both sat in a somber silence of several seconds before Candace spoke again. "Encourage your son to work on maintaining his relationship with his grandmother. Help her with things that he can help with. Show her with his actions that he loves her. You can help by showing him how." Candace sighed. "That's the best I can offer you . . . thoughts and prayers."

Harold rose from his chair. "Thank you, Candace. Sorry for taking up your time."

Candace stood up as well. Ignoring social distancing recommendations, she reached out to pat his arm. "Any time, Harold."

Irene Faulkner had left a curious voice mail on Harold's mobile phone. Something about the School on the Green, a former elementary school that had been boarded up for decades. He decided best to go talk to her in person. He found Irene in a somewhat calmer state than when he had left her.

"The hospital called," she said. "One of the nurses talked to me. Said that Arney's vital signs were improving."

"That's good to know."

"Good of them to communicate with me."

"Arney's in the new converted garage area."

The information disturbed Irene. "Oh, dear, in that drafty place?"

"I was inside. It's a lot better than you might expect. Inside, you can't tell that anything is temporary. Or a garage." Time to move the conversation forward. "You sent me a message about the old School on the Green."

"Yes. The Brownlow Company has bought the building from the school district. They're converting it to one of those business incubators."

Harold nodded knowingly. "What do they mean – incubators?"

"Dividing everything into small spaces, usually convertible, where new businesses just getting started can have an office address, access to common services, like printing, that they can offer for a very low rental. Sometimes it's very temporary, someone can rent a desk and a little space for a few days." She continued, "They're going to be adapting the space and they want some vending machines."

"They're just getting started? Little premature for vending machines," was Harold's opinion.

"No, vending machines are one of the first things they want – an income stream. That's one way they're planning to pay for the remodeling. The carpenters and plasterers and plumbers and electricians will all have an appetite. Someone from the company opened the building this morning and will have a design crew starting work on the premises. I told them we don't have any new machines in inventory and they said they'd take what we have – all the better in case there might be an accident during construction and a machine gets damaged."

"Well, that makes some sense," Harold admitted.

Irene continued, "I called the delivery guys and they can take any of the machines we have in house over by this afternoon. I'd like for you to meet the Brownlow company people over there and make some decisions about getting some machines up and running."

Harold's head was reeling at the speed with which the new development was being set in motion. "I can do that. First I'd better check to see what we have ready to go back in the warehouse."

With his phone Harold took pictures of the existing inventory he thought might best fit the situation, and headed for the School on the Green. En route, he couldn't resist calling Sabrina. "There's some good news for business in The Green," hc teased her.

"Spill it. I'm always ready for good news."

"Someone has found a use for the old School on the Green

elementary school."

"That building! It's been closed for years. They're going to convert it into senior apartments like they did the old Benton school?"

"Better. Something quite different. An incubator for new businesses. And they want vending machines from the beginning, even before they begin construction."

"That will be exciting, to be in on the beginning."

"Yeah, I think they're crazy, but as long as the color of their money is green..."

The Brownlow people wanted two sets of vending machines, one for cold drinks and one for snacks, one set at the front doors and the second set at the rear doors, which would lead to the parking lot. "Don't bolt them down too tight," one of the company men advised. "We might want to move them later."

Harold said, "Yeah, but tight enough that they don't grow legs!"

By late afternoon the vending machines were in place, waiting for temporary electrical service to be restored to the building. Harold bumped elbows with three of the company men as they locked the doors for the night.

Leaving The Green, Harold realized that he still had up on the dashboard the instruction sheets he'd forgotten to deliver to Dayl at the shop. He expected that Dayl would have gone home by now. He thought of continuing home himself, but his conscience told him to take the extra minutes to stop at the shop so the instructions would be there for Dayl in the morning. He was doing all he could to try to support Sabrina, and the kids, and now to support Irene and Arney ... He let himself quietly in the back door. Most of the lights were off but there was enough ambient light for him to see his way through the shop. What Harold hadn't imagined was finding Dayl still in the shop, in a rocking chair he had pulled up to the front window. Knitting.

Clearly, Dayl hadn't envisioned, either, the unanticipated arrival of someone at the back door. When he saw Harold's figure, he froze, caught in the act. At his feet a project bag with the slogan KEEP CLAM AND CURRY ON, in his lap the finished portion of a colorful scarf, and in his hands a pair of light-colored bamboo knitting needles. Number Tens. Wordless, Harold stared at Dayl. Dismayed, Dayl stared back. They both spoke at the same time.

"Well, now you know my secret." Dayl pulled his mask up from around his throat. "I'm making this for your mother. It's a surprise," he quickly added.

"I didn't know you were a knitter." Harold reached for his mask, tangled in his collar. "That's quite a secret."

"It's amazing what you can pick up on YouTube. I just started. I figured while I was here I might as well learn something."

Harold pulled up a nearby rocker and sank onto the cushion, grateful for an unexpected chance to relax. "I thought your wife was a quilter."

"She was. Although she did know how to knit. Taught our granddaughter, Tressa, some of the basic steps. Not that Tressa knits now. And, not a word, yet. She doesn't know I've started. Let me surprise her. When the time is right."

"How is that granddaughter? I hear they put her to work at the hospital."

"They did. She's there every day. I'm a little worried about her online classes. I don't think she's touched her computer."

"It's hard to keep Nathan focused on his remote learning."

Dayl started to put his knit project into a plastic bag. "And now there seems to be a young man in the picture. I don't know how she managed to meet him, but when this Pandemic is over, I'm worried she may not go back to college."

Both men jumped at a light tap on the front door.

"It's Louise Newquist," Dayl explained. "I was waiting for her. Sabrina said to expect her."

As Dayl moved to open the door it seemed to Harold that Dayl had finally added a little weight to his lanky frame.

Mrs. Newquist stepped inside. "Thank you so much. I'm almost finished." She took a small bag Dayl handed to her. "How much do I owe you?"

Dayl consulted a piece of paper lying on the cash register. "Ten dollars and fifty-six cents."

"I'm sorry I'm late. I didn't expect the repair people to be so late in getting my car back." She stepped farther into the store and peered into the darkened interior. "I wonder if we'll ever be able to gather again like we used to?"

"You know," Harold speculated, "Sabrina misses those gatherings, too." He rose from the rocker. "I'm Harold. Mr. Sabrina," he offered. "Hang in there. Sabrina will be welcoming everyone back as soon as she can."

SABRINA

Chapter Fifteen

S abrina was listening to Harold's basketball game. Not that she had any interest in basketball, or the game, but she would not be able to talk to Harold until the game was over.

She had come to enjoy their late night stairway chats. She at the top of the stairs, her life-time Romeo on a stool at the bottom. They would conclude their talk reluctantly, she off to her lonely king-size bed in the master bedroom and Harold seeking sleep on his lumpy basement couch. Their only kisses were blown and the only hugs were embraces they gave to themselves. Rather than separate, they lingered long over their conversations, trying to think of one more thing they needed to talk about. Sometimes nothings.

"Mrs. Newquist came in the shop late this afternoon. After hours. Dayl had stayed, he was waiting for her. She's been working on her project since before the Pandemic. Always seems to need just one more hank of thread in some special color or weight in order to finish."

"What's she knitting?"

"It's secret. And it's not knitting, it's needlepoint."

"Something going on with her and Mr. Carruthers?"

Sabrina paused. "Not that I know of, what makes you think that?"

Harold was slow to respond. "She was just so . . . coy."

"She moved here from Florida about a year and a half ago. She probably hasn't been able to make many friends before the Pandemic."

They were both silent for several moments before Sabrina spoke again. "Nana tells me that Dayl's granddaughter has a new boyfriend. You heard anything about that?"

"Not a word."

"Nana says it's someone at the hospital. She thinks it's one of the doctors."

"Well, she's a pretty girl. When she's around, she's the only thing Nathan has eyes for."

"Letting him get a dog is probably a good thing . . . ," Sabrina was only slowly overcoming her resistance to the addition of an animal to the household , " . . . a college girl would be a little old for him."

"Exactly. Too much upkeep, too," said Harold. "A dog should give him something else to think about. I think he's going to bring his new pet home tomorrow."

"How much is it going to cost?"

"I don't understand it, but the shelter is waiving the fees."

"Are they giving him credit for all the walking he's been doing?"

"Maybe something like that. It's okay by me. He said there would be some papers for me to sign."

Sabrina was running out of things she wanted to discuss with Harold and the hour was late. "Elsbeth has been fever free for six days now. They would probably let her back in school."

"She'll be excited about that. We can let Nathan come back home. Give Nana a break."

"I'm not too far behind her. In fact, this might be your last night in the basement." She got up from the steps and stood in the kitchen doorway.

"I'm ready for that."

She blew him a kiss.

Sabrina had read everything she could find on the internet about sterilizing the environment. Not only was Sabrina happy that she had been fever free – for five days now – she was pleased that she seemed to have a better reserve of energy. In between contacts with the shop and answering e-mails, she rubbed cleaning wipes on every door knob and every other touchable surface. It was as clean as their little home had ever been, and she thought she'd been a good home manager all along.

Laurin and Sabrina had talked every day. Laurin always asked about Sabrina's symptoms, but Sabrina always fibbed a little, tried to minimize the worst, but not be too optimistic about the betterment for fear of a relapse. "Is it possible to get this thing more than once, like the flu?"

Laurin didn't know the answer. "I hope it's not like catching a cold."

Today Sabrina decided to tell Laurin the truth. "I'm really getting better. Haven't had a fever for five days now."

Laurin released a sign of relief. "I'm so glad to hear that. It'd be dreadful if you were in quarantine on Sidewalk Sale Days. The sidewalk thing has just exploded all over town. And it was all your idea, Sabrina."

Even in quarantine Sabrina had come to a growing awareness that something bigger than just her sidewalk sale might be going on. But Covid and her business had kept her nose to the grindstone. Dayl was a trooper. And finding him and his willingness to pitch right in was beyond lucky. Without Dayl there would have been no way to be this ready for the sale. And Harold was re-writing the Romeo part. But Sabrina had no idea what was happening beyond the four walls and her mobile phone. Even Harold, and Dayl too, at the very eye of the storm, weren't seeing the rainbow yet.

"Well, It's all due to you. Everyone is getting excited. There are stories and ads all over the newspapers and television," said Laurin. "Your friend Jamma is beside herself. I hear the Chamber is going to produce a video of every store that's having a sidewalk sale."

"Every store or just the Chamber members?"

Laurin laughed. "Every store, a promotional video for the whole town. Of course, they hope the non-members will get on board and maybe even join."

The next call was from Dayl. "Mrs. Newquist phoned and wanted to know if we have someone who will make a sofa pillow out of her needlepoint. She has six finished projects."

"Yes, we do. We have to send them out of town and it takes a while to get them back. Costs a pretty penny, too. I'll give her a call."

"That's all right," Dayl almost interrupted. "I told her I would find out and call her back."

And the next call was again from Dayl. "There's a yarn salesman here with a van load of yarn that I didn't know you had ordered. He wants to talk to you."

"Okay?" Sabrina said dubiously.

"Mrs. Harkins?" came a strong voice. "Sam Ballinger here." She recognized his voice. "It sounded like such a great idea when you told me. About your sidewalk sale to sort of break the Covid's economic fever. So to speak. We tried to figure out how we could support and help you with what you are doing." Sabrina didn't think Sam had paused to take a breath before he continued, "Wholesale Yarns doesn't want your sidewalk sale to fall short on inventory. We've just got a shipment of yarn from the Falklands for knitters who favor natural colors..."

"I'm already overextended. I can't afford..."

"No worries. This is consignment inventory. You only pay for what you sell in the sidewalk sale. There's some fantastic new yarns from Canada. You'll love them. We brought things in from all over." He even said, "It's a rainbow." They talked colors, and fibers, and feel for a minute. "Aren't you about at the end of your quarantine?"

"Matter of fact, I am," Sabrina fudged a little. She reached in her pants pocket to feel for her car keyfob. "I'll be down at the shop in twenty minutes. I can't believe you are here." She clicked off her phone and called to Elsbeth. "Grab your jacket, we're going to the store."

It took a bit longer than twenty minutes. Elsbeth was quite excited – her first trip out of the house for days. "I miss my friends. Will I get to go back to school?"

"Yes." Sabrina promised and sent Elsbeth back to her room to get her mask. Sabrina chose a route that took her past most of the businesses on Huron Street. She was stunned at what she saw. Floored. Most had large notices of upcoming Sidewalk Sales. Some were crudely drawn on shop windows. Others were obviously quite professional. All were colorful. A large van sat in front of the yarn store. In enticing letters on the side of the van that she could see were the words FOLLOW ME TO YOUR LYS. She had to stop her car to read the message on the back: YOUR LOCAL YARN SHOP. The accompanying illustrations were cascades of colorful yarns with happy sheep and goofy llamas. One of the llamas was saying "Your Grandmother said you should knit something." Sabrina smiled at that. When she coasted past Elizabeth's Yarn Place, she could see Dayl and Greg and a couple more people she didn't know jockeying boxes through the front door. Her first thought was . . . no, she was still too overwhelmed to collect a first thought. Sabrina turned at the corner and then turned again into the alley behind the store. There were a few wide places in the alley that offered short-term, temporary parking. She might be lucky.

But barely. In one of the spaces she recognized Chip Quinn's car. None of the men looked up at Sabrina's entry through the back door. Their attention was centered on a large stack of boxes in the middle of the floor. With one arm Chip was hanging on to several skeins of a pink and orange yarn with flecks of gold. Dayl was concentrating on skeins of denim blue. The first to notice Sabrina's arrival, Sam straightened up to greet her. He reached to shake hands, and corrected to a fist bump. Sabrina noticed that Sam was wearing a sweater that featured a line of elephants, each elephant's trunk holding onto the tail of the elephant in front. She made him turn around so she could see the full circle. "Who knit your sweater?"

Sam stood up taller. "I did," he said emphatically.

Both Dayl and Chip also straightened up to look at Sam. And his sweater. He knit.

"You did a beautiful job." Sabrina pulled her mobile phone out of its pouch and noticed she had a call from Harold. She put the phone back; she would answer the call later.

"How could I work in a warehouse full of yarn and not learn how to use it?"

"You ought to put that out on the display circuit. Is the pattern available?"

"Not yet. We are working it up."

Dayl and Chip had quit staring at Sam and were looking at each other.

Sam pulled an invoice from one of the boxes. "Some of these yarns are from a new supplier. Northwoods from Southern Manitoba in Canada. Valle Vista from the low Sierras in California. Small businesses from all over. Just like yours. They started out as a bunch of sheep ranchers for the meat industry who fell in love with what could be done with wool," he said, kind of to remind himself of the path he too was on: "Entrepreneurs, you gotta love 'em." He handed Sabrina a skein of yellow, gold and white.

Sabrina turned the skein over, felt a single strand with her fingers. "It's very good of your company to support my shop with, like credit, for more inventory."

"Ma'am, the whole industry is indebted to you. Yarn shops all across the country are following your example. Even some whole towns, like Overlake, are having sidewalk sales days, all other kinds of so-called non-essential businesses. Independent book stores, mom-and-pop hardware stores, kitchen stores. You name it."

Still not quite understanding the bigger picture, Sabrina thought to add, "Still it was good of you to make a personal delivery."

"Haven't you heard? This is big. I drove all night. I'm going to send our lot dye expert to help on the days of the sale. He's really good. A knitter too. We were afraid regular shipping might not get this here quickly enough. Besides, I wanted to see for myself. And meet you. Be sure to share plenty of pix." Sam started for the door. "I've got some other business to take care of," he waved. "We'll be in touch." Sabrina thought 'When does he breathe?'

Chip bought every skein of the pink-orange-gold yarn, and left, a happy shopper. Dayl bought four skeins of denim blue, a bargain because Sabrina gave him an employee discount. Sabrina asked Dayl to close out for the day. She was overwhelmed, and realized that there still was a lot to do before the sale.

At home, Elsbeth popped out of the car, headed for the side porch door into the kitchen, and raced back with a scream. "There's something on the porch." Sabrina could see nothing, but she had no doubt something had terrified Elsbeth. "It's moving," Elsbeth shrieked, and grabbed her mother around the upper leg. At the sound of another vehicle, Sabrina was relieved to see Harold's van come hastily sliding into the driveway.

Harold almost fell out of the van. "I've been trying to call you," Harold yelled and hastened to catch Sabrina. Nathan slowly slid out of the passenger seat, holding back.

"Elsbeth says there is something on the porch." Trembling, Elsbeth held onto Sabrina.

"Yep. There is. It's Nathan's pet. I've been trying to call you to give you a heads-up here."

Sabrina had reached the porch door and had a good view inside the porch. She stopped abruptly. "It's a – raccoon!"

"Yes. He didn't tell us, did he?" Harold turned with a direct look at Nathan, who was lifting a wire cage from the van.

Sabrina was peering closely at the raccoon. The creature was scuttling awkwardly around the edge of the porch. "What's the matter with its back leg?"

Harold had reached Sabrina's side. "Broken leg in the accident on Strawn OverPass. This is the raccoon that was all over the news three or four weeks ago. The shelter docs did the best they could, but they decided they could never release it back to the wild. And in the meantime, Nathan had gotten acquainted with the raccoon. Gave it a name, Sweeney, after the shelter guy." Harold's demeanor bordered on apologetic. "So when we agreed that Nathan could have a pet, Sweeney was what he wanted." Harold put his arm around Sabrina's shoulder. "That was why there were no fees."

"I can understand why. They should be paying us." She watched Nathan lug the wire cage up to the porch door.

"The shelter even offered Nathan a cage, but it was pretty little, so we went to the pet store. I tried to call you," he said again. Harold gave her another shoulder squeeze, hoping it might help. "You look like you're kind of wiped out. How about Elsbeth and I go find some carry-out food. What would you like?"

"That Thai garlic chicken was pretty good. I couldn't smell it but I could sure sense it."

"Thai Palace it is. Come on, Elsbeth. I need you to help me."

Cautiously, Sabrina followed Nathan on to the porch and helped him coax Sweeney into the cage. "Thanks, Mom. Love you." Sabrina wasn't totally won over, yet.

Except for the raccoon, good luck followed Sabrina for the next few days. For starters, every weather report predicted a mild, maybe even pleasant run of temperatures for the sidewalk sale days. Nana was alerted to having Elsbeth with her for the sale. In return, Sabrina invited Nana to have an advance look at the new yarns. Nana was delighted. She took three skeins home.

On Wednesday before the Sidewalk Sale Days event Sabrina woke up in a panic mode. She called Laurin as early as she thought she could without interrupting Laurin's at home activities, breakfast for her law enforcement husband, distributing her children for the day.

"Laurin, I feel okay, but I'm so depressed. I think it's covid-fatigue."

"Don't be pessimistic. It's going to be fantastic. This whole town's going to be . . . well, there may be a few surprises we didn't expect."

"Like what?"

"Oh . . . just things no one ever thought could happen."

"Real customers?" Sabrina asked hopefully.

"That, too," said Lauren with a laugh.

"Is some movie star coming to town that I haven't heard of. Will Bill Murray be helping people make their color choices? Bill Murray in his custom-knit sweater?"

"No, not Bill Murray," Laurin laughed. "If Bill Murray comes to town, he'll head straight for the golf links."

"You're right about that. I guess I need to calm down. Tell Irwin hello."

"Irwin says hello back. Says he'll see you tomorrow. I gotta run now. Patrick is in school today. The little one goes to day-care, but I may have to borrow your Nana."

"I'll send you her phone number in an e-mail." Clicking off, Sabrina was puzzled: what did Laurin mean that Irwin would see her tomorrow?

Sabrina picked up her yellow notepad and headed for her car. She had nothing written below the heading "Sidewalk Sales Check List. But she hoped to have a good start before Dayl showed up at 11 am. Sabrina tried to greet Dayl with a bright smile, but she was sure he could see it was wallpaper.

Dayl came in through the rear door, mask already on his nose. He was patting his shirt pocket. "Dang. Must have left my phone at home." He looked at the yellow notepad lying on the table. "Got all the marching orders laid out?"

"I'm working on it. I'll ask you to look it over for anything I've missed . . . I'll make a copy."

They both bent over the worksheets; a quick tapping at the front door brought up their heads simultaneously. Tressa, waving a mobile phone in one hand made the motion of opening the door with her other hand. Closest to the door, Sabrina jumped to her feet.

"Grandpa! How can I call you if your phone is at home on the kitchen table? I found it when I went looking for you."

Dayl took the phone from Tressa and began checking for messages. "I see you have been trying to call me." He looked out the front window at her car. "I didn't recognize your car with all your things unloaded," he quipped.

"You didn't notice last night?"

"But I do see you've already got it reloaded. Who's your passenger?'

"Come on out and I'll introduce him, but you already know who it is. Jay. Your friend Vince Garretson's son. He's got a walking boot on his right leg, but he can't drive a car yet. I wanted to tell you that we're going to Metropole. I'm taking the day off."

"It's about time you're taking a break. Hopefully none of us will test positive, but we're all suffering from Covid-fatigue."

Startled, Sabrina quickly added, "That's what I told my friend this morning when I started out feeling a little down."

"What did she say?" Tressa asked.

"She told me to fake it until we make it, and to smile a little." She gave Tressa a big stretchy smile as Tressa walked out the door. Sabrina couldn't be sure, at the angle of view she had, but she thought that when Tressa got into the car Jay leaned over to kiss Tressa on her neck below the mask. Maybe she needed to start working on a wedding shawl someday. Nathan might take it hard. But, hey, he had Sweeney, what more could a kid want besides a daredevil, lucky in life, raccoon? If it was to be a wedding shawl it had to be out of one of the glorious yarns Sam Ballinger had left. After Sidewalk Sale days.

Although she knew in advance that Harold was officially taking a day off from work, it seemed strange that when he rolled out of bed – their king-sized bed in the master bedroom – he dressed in what he called civilian clothing. At the breakfast table he scanned his mobile phone for messages. He glanced up at Sabrina. "Here's some good news. They took my boss off the ventilator last night."

"Good news indeed. Thank God," said Sabrina.

Nathan had his eyes on his mother all through breakfast and seemed to be on the verge of saying something to her. When he spoke he thanked her – again – for letting him keep Sweeney, the raccoon. It sure could eat the kibble. When Harold left to take Nathan to school, Nathan called back. "See you later, Mom." Sabrina saw a quick hand movement from Harold, a warning that Nathan should be quiet. Her 'boys' were always talking in man-code.

To synchronize with the other merchants, Sabrina had decided to officially open at 9 am on the first day of Sidewalk Sale, instead of the usual 11 am. With Elsbeth in tow, she bolted out of the house at 8:15. When she dropped Elsbeth off at Nana's, Elsbeth had the same good-bye message as Nathan. "See you later, Mom." And Nana also made the quiet sign.

Passing a large gasoline station, Sabrina thought she caught a glimpse of Sam Ballinger's FOLLOW ME TO YOUR LYS van, but by the time she drove around the block it was gone. Harold drove into the parking lot behind Sabrina and they walked to the shop together. Dayl had beat them there and was moving folding tables and merchandise racks out to the sidewalk.

As far as Sabrina could see up and down the block, almost every business had at least one table set up outside on the sidewalk. With only intangibles to sell, the insurance office between her shop and the Finest of the Caribbean had some helium-filled balloons and a sign WE'RE OPEN FOR BUSINESS.

For Sabrina, the morning quickly got busy. And stranger. Chip Quinn arrived, pulling three wooden folding rockers, and a two-sided sandwich board in a folding wagon. At the end of one of Sabrina's tables he unfolded the rocking chairs. "My brother in West Virginia makes these folding rockers. Sells them as fast as the varnish dries. I've got one to leave at your shop." Chip set up the sandwich board and wrote a chalk message on both sides: 'Join the Good Ole Boys Knitting League. Free membership'. Then he sat down in the middle rocker and opened a knitting bag. Sabrina was too stunned to ask, but he was making a rather large object of the pink-orange-gold yarn he had claimed several days ago. Dayl was soon in one of the rockers with his denim colored yarn, at work on what appeared to be a simple scarf. But he was about to get too busy to keep up work on his scarf she thought. And caught herself: 'Dayl knits?!'

Mrs. Newquist made her way from the municipal parking lot across the street, a large brown paper grocery bag in her hands. Glancing at Dayl, she made her way directly toward Sabrina. "I've finished my needlepoint projects. You said you can send them off to someone who can make them into sofa pillows?"

"Certainly. Let's see what you have." She started to take the brown paper bag from Mrs. Newquist's hands; Mrs. Newquist pulled the bag closer to her side.

"Let's go inside," she said in a tone that was demanding. "I have six finished panels. I want three sofa pillows."

Sabrina motioned to Dayl that she was going inside the shop with Mrs. Newquist. Inside Mrs. Newquist took three panels from the bag and laid them on the table. Sabrina looked admiringly at the three floral panels. "I'm confused. You have six panels and you want three pillows?"

"Yes. They will be double-sided." Mrs. Newquist glanced through the window at Dayl and Chip. "I don't want anyone to see them." she removed three more panels and laid them on the table wrong side up. "You'll see them when you send them to the finisher." Slowly, dramatically, she turned the panels over and laid them in a row on the table.

Sabrina was speechless for several moments. "You naughty girl," she told Mrs. Newquist. Laid out in order the three panels portrayed a lounging, nearly nude, he could be nude, dark-haired, young man.

"Those are for me," Mrs. Newquist coyly explained. "When I have company, all they will see are roses and tulips and daffodils and green leaves and fernery."

"You naughty girl," Sabrina repeated, otherwise speechless. She hastened to put them all back inside the brown paper bag, along with the business card with the name of Louise Newquist to help identify the needlepoints, as if worked tapestries of a nearly nude man would be easy to forget. When she next looked, Mrs. Newquist had gone outside and was sitting in the middle rocking chair. Chip had put a pair of knitting needles in her hands. Sabrina could overhear Chip talking to Mrs. Newquist. "There's nothing to it, Lolly. It's just two sticks and a piece of string."

— § —

The morning was busy but not rushed. When there was more than one customer at the tables, Dayl put his project aside and joined her. One young woman was wearing a sweater in a pattern that looked familiar to Sabrina. Most of the front of the sweater was a large cat. Something clicked in Sabrina's mind and she blurted out to the young woman, "You're Mrs. Reynolds granddaughter!"

The young woman stepped back, "How did you know?"

"I remember Mrs. Reynolds knitting that sweater. How is she? I miss her coming into the shop."

"She's fine, but she went to live temporarily with her sister."

Sabrina pulled out her mobile phone. "Would you mind if I took a picture of the sweater? Could I be in touch with Mrs. Reynolds? Get her permission to put it on my blog? I need your permission, too. Would that be okay?"

"I'll send her an e-mail." The granddaughter tried to pose in a manner that best revealed the pattern on the sweater.

"Thank you," Sabrina said, pocketing her mobile phone. "Tell her we miss her, will be glad when she moves back. And tell her she did a terrific job with that sweater."

About 10:45 am Harold disappeared without telling her where he was going. She was almost too busy to notice.

At 11 am they all suddenly heard the blare of marching music. All the meandering shoppers stopped in their tracks and looked about confused. Now curious, Dayl, Mrs. Newquist and Chip all stood up. Sabrina scanned the surroundings but Harold had not returned

"It's coming from around the corner," someone called out.

And from around that corner onto Huron Street came the Overlake High School Marching Band, socially distanced from curb to curb, playing their victory song. Tight on their heels, recognizable by Sabrina because he was wearing the same clothing, was KØCBTO from the candy store, a handi-talky at his lips. He was quite at ease directing traffic, including a two-person television crew trying to focus on the flashing legs of the leading cheerleader.

Visible only after the band had almost passed was Nana's sedan, bedecked with balloons and ribbons, Elsbeth waving wildly from the passenger window. On foot, Nathan and Alford walked at each side of the sedan. Anna was followed by a solitary figure in a clown suit, doing spins and whirls and gyrations on a unicycle like nobody's business.

"That's Vince! Vince Garretson," shouted Dayl. "Nobody can ride like Vince. And he's old. Like me!" Sabrina recognized jealousy with a little admiration mixed in when she heard it. And she almost giggled.

Keeping a safe distance was Tressa's Volkswagen, her passenger, Jay Garretson, who waved weakly as he kept a jealous eye on the unicycle. A crew from a rival television station kept pace with the unicycle, perhaps wanting to be on the spot to record a spectacular crash. The cyclist taunted them, rolling within inches before wheeling madly away.

The sounds of the band receded, to be followed by chaotic calypso melodies, the unmistakable rhythms of a steel drum band. On the sides of their food truck were colorful banners proclaiming COMING SOON CARIBBEAN CANTEEN. Greg, clad in an outrageous floral shirt, was behind the wheel. In a multicolored mummu, Jamma crossed back and forth passing out discount sales coupons. She was obviously having a great time and, as Jamma always was, she was obviously working hard.

There was more. An Overlake ambulance made way for a vintage convertible. Draped in red scarves, Sally Voyles was seated high on the rear seat. She wielded a giant pair of knitting needles. Banners on the sides announced RED SCARVES AGAINST CANCER.

A jeep with more than a half-dozen antennas was next. Riding shotgun for the driver was a large tan dog, a set of custom-designed ear phones around the back of his neck. Two men on foot, each with an antenna sticking up from his back-pack, passed out lollipops and encouraged the crowd to come visit the candy store. They were joined by several walking, and talking, hams.

And next in line was the colorful FOLLOW ME TO YOUR LYS van, which Sabrina had thought she had seen earlier at the gasoline station, driven by a man Sabrina did not recognize but assumed was the dye lot specialist; Sam Ballinger, wearing his sweater with the circle of elephants, was walking alongside.

When the Overlake Vending Company van appeared, Sabrina looked in vain for Harold; she assumed the woman behind the wheel was Irene Faulkner. Irene was waving, as best she could while driving. Drawing even with the yarn shop, she switched hands to point directly at Sabrina with a big smile. Sabrina watched her smile and say 'Thank you'. The crowd was drowning out pretty much every conversation.

Flashing red and blue lights, an Overlake police car with a wailing siren took over. The police vehicle was followed by the Overlake High School Marching Band. Again. Sabrina caught sight of Harold, handi-talky at his mouth. Somehow he had led the band around the block to return to bring up the rear. He gave the band director a wave-off and began to move toward Sabrina.

Laurin suddenly appeared at Sabrina's side and was waving wildly at the driver of the police car, and his passenger, Patrick, wearing a green plaid Irish tam. "Isn't this exciting? She shouted in Sabrina's ear. "It was all I could do to keep from telling you yesterday." Irwin, driving the police car, was waving at Sabrina.

"Who's running your shop?"

"Mabel. She's the lady I bought the shop from. She's having a ball, coming out of retirement."

The band members cleared a path for a state highway patrol car that eased along the curb and came to a stop in front of the yarn shop.

The parade vehicles had all stopped in the street just beyond the shop. The drivers and walkers were hastily converging in front of Elizabeth's Yarn Place. They all wore masks and tried to maintain a social distance as best they could. Many of them were looking at Sabrina, who wondered why most of the attention was focused on her. She looked frantically for Harold.

Greg, in his flamboyant shirt, was almost running toward Sabrina, but he did not slow down as he came within speaking range. He flew on past, stopping only when he almost collided with Harold.

Harold stopped as well, took his hand-held transceiver from in front of his face and held it out for Greg's observation; he did not allow Greg to touch the handi-talky. Sabrina smiled. From the distance it appeared that Harold was making another convert to the amateur radio community.

Laurin, her gaze transfixed, could not take her eyes off Greg. "Where did he buy that shirt? I'll bet I could sell tropical shirts in my store."

Stepping out of the patrol car was the mayor. He was immediately surrounded by the television camera crews. "Would Sabrina Harkins, owner of Elizabeth's Yarn Place, please step forward? Where is Sabrina?"

"Sabrina. Sabrina. Sabrina," came an echo from the crowd.

Dayl gave Sabrina another nudge. Where was Harold?

"Sabrina Harkins," continued the mayor, his voice rising over the rooftops, "the governor regrets not being here in person on this momentous day, but has given me the authority to proclaim that in recognition of her passion, innovation, and indomitable spirit, three of the hallmarks of forward looking businesses, as she envisioned and made a reality of sidewalk sales which quickly proved inspirational and uplifting to others as she continued to parent and run her small business from her Covid quarantine, I hereby declare Sabrina Harkins of Elizabeth's Yarn Place in the City of Overlake, to be the Entrepreneur of the Year."

The crowd went wild. Two people with television cameras moved in closer to Sabrina.

The mayor adlibbed still shuffling over-long speech notes:

"May today be an inspiration and a blessing to all. May everyone who has been touched by Covid, themselves, their friends, their family, our community, be strong and courageous and follow the path that Sabrina has shown us all." The gathered crowd softened the celebration for a moment. They could tell the old politician had asked for a truly heartfelt blessing. No one, but the mayor, knew that his own mother was gone to Covid just the past week. Covid was everywhere, and anywhere.

Sabrina hardly had words to respond. Harold suddenly appeared behind her, pushed her forward and said over her shoulder, "Sabrina Harkins is honored to receive this award. Please give the governor her thanks and gratitude. Thank you, Mr. Mayor." Harold put his arm firmly around Sabrina's waist to keep her steady on her feet, to keep her from falling over. Gobsmacked. "You're the Queen of the Sidewalk Sales," Harold whispered, and to the crowd said, "Please thank everyone and tell them good job, well done." He moved his arm in a sweeping gesture. "Thank you all for coming." Sabrina never knew her Romeo to be so eloquent.

Sabrina felt her knees buckle. Before she could fall, Chip slid a rocker that his brother's small business made, whispering in her ear. "A Throne for the Queen".

Epilogue, and yet American Prologue too

Small businesses are the warp and weft of America. They feed families and fulfill dreams. They drive innovation, whether born of necessity or opportunity. They are the sibling force and strong protector of liberty and freedom. They are work, sweat and blood and fever and thrill and success. And failure and rebirth too. Small businesses are, as Jamma knew and Harold is growing to understand as Sabrina reminds us all, as American as America can be.

Closure

The sidewalk sale went very well. Better, actually, than Sabrina had expected or hoped. As it did for every other business who had found a way to join in. It was a celebration of the best of small business. A return to roots, and a renewal. A Sidewalk Sale across America.

For Sabrina, it vindicated her beliefs about her abilities and business and brought new skills and confidence. Old customers were glad for a chance to return. New customers found her too. Sabrina knew that she was leaving old worries behind. And that there would be a whole set of new. Such is life. Sabrina, and the business, would continue to grow.

Harold saw a new Sabrina. It strengthened him. And lightened his worries too. Now if he could only get Sweeney to stop trying to tear up the porch. The short term promised repairs. Maybe he could use them to pass some things on to Nathan at the same time.

Nathan had already figured out, to Harold's amazement, how to use the yarn shop's Facebook page to Facebooks version of livestream some of Sabrina's sidewalk sale specials mixing in a couple of on-street customer interviews. He was on the laptop most of the day. He did a particularly excellent job of showcasing the colors of Sabrina's yarn inventory. It caught Sam Ballinger's eye. Sabrina thought she was catching a glimpse of Nathan's future. He was, after all, growing up. And she understood that they both were ready.

But Elsbeth, well Elsbeth was going to be in a child's world for a little while longer. As long as Sabrina could keep her. There would be more floppy eared knit rabbits, a few soft knit cats, a pumpkin throw pillow, from Nana, and many brightly colored knit sweaters and Chameleon scarves before it would be time for her to become a teenager.

Dayl, with the able direction of Sgt. Knitman and his friends in the Good Ole Boys Knitting League, had knit a Chameleon scarf of the most wonderful merino for Elsbeth. It wasn't quite pinks. But it wasn't quite reds either. It was some eye catching new color he somehow found there in between.

As for Nana, and Tressa, we don't yet know if Dayl or Jay will become life fixtures. But there is room to imagine.

And the ham nets would keep on doing what ham nets do: "Anyone got their ear's on? I hear that Jim-Pop's is doing a happy hour on banana and strawberry shakes. Going to be crowd. KD8TKLT"

The pandemic isn't beaten. Yet. There is always the possibility for this, and other dangers, ahead. But there is promise. There is promise and hope to work toward, and to work for.

Stop in to say "Hi!" to Sabrina next time you are out shopping – she is hard at work on her share of 'the Dream' somewhere you know.

BOOKS BY THIS AUTHOR

Mediation Survivor's Handbook

Mediation preparation book for the non-professional mediation participants.

I Kneeded It

A collection of poetry generated by the author's need for knee replacement surgery. A guide.

Emergency, No-Guilt Hot Chocolate

Prose culminating in a wonderful recipe for hot chocolate without sugar.

ART OF THE BOOK

This work is short enough, and hopefully sweet enough, that there is no table of contents. And certainly no index. Garamond font is employed throughout for Please enjoy.

To our beta readers: we are grateful for the suggestions and comments you have made, and apologize for bringing you into the process so late in the game. Especially helpful was the insight from a fellow radio ham, ACØKN, Jim Cessna, and a cast of *beta* readers including author Ann Friedman.

Covers, both front and back, were designed and the photographs included were taken by Britt Nichols with rendering assistance by Tatro Design of Lawrence, Kansas.

This book, consisting of my original 40,000 words would never have left my computer except for the vision of Britt Nichols, an editor extraordinaire, who added another 10,000 well-chosen words in expertly-crafted paragraphs. We share a joint conviction that small business owners, either as a sole employee working alone, or with a small crew, have the skill, guts, courage, knowledge, enterprise, determination and optimism (perhaps out of necessity or desperation) to drive the American economy to a new normal, a Better Normal.

CQ, CQ, CQ, THIS IS KDØVQO CALLING CQ.

STOP!

Before you go to the trouble of getting in touch with me to explain to me how I've got the call signs all wrong, let me tell you how impossible it is to find fictional call signs for fictional characters.

Radio hams are rightfully possessive about their call signs. Thier call signs are their names. The call sign becomes their ham radio identity – on-air and off.

Call sign prefixes of one or two letters are determined by the International Telecommunications Union. Following the prefix, United States Federal Communications Commission assigns a number, which indicates a geographic region, and then a suffix consisting up to three letters. There aren't very many two letter suffixes in use. Most two letter suffixes are silent key. Amateur radio license holders can request a specific suffix, called a vanity license, which may be their initials, or the call sign previously held by a parent or mentor. I hold my own license, KDØVQO. My parents were hams first licensed in California and later in Kansas City, MO.

Thanks for your contact. Clear on your final.

ELEVATOR PITCH

Sabrina Harkins found herself in the fight of her life to save her family and her business, and their futures, from the Covid-19 Pandemic and the economic ravages to follow when she re-discovered and re-purposed a tried-and-true business idea to a new future to achieve Covid health guidelines: Why not hold a simple Sidewalk Sale – and if everyone joined in it would be the biggest small business coming out success story all across America, and . . .

Why not a SIDEWALK SALE across AMERICA? If there is going to be a "New Normal", why not make it a Better Normal? Overcoming the Covid Pandemic takes grit, determination, perseverance. It takes all of us.

Made in the USA
Coppell, TX
12 April 2021